Sadie Rose
AND THE CHAMPION SHARPSHOOTER

A SADIE ROSE ADVENTURE

Sadie Rose
AND THE
CHAMPION
SHARPSHOOTER

Hilda Stahl

CROSSWAY BOOKS • WHEATON, ILLINOIS
A DIVISION OF GOOD NEWS PUBLISHERS

Cover illustration: Kathy Kulin

First printing, 1991

Printed in the United States of America

Library of Congress Cataloging-in-Publication Data
Stahl, Hilda.
    Sadie Rose and the champion sharpshooter / Hilda Stahl.
        p.   cm. — (The Prairie family adventure series))
    Summary: Twelve year-old Sadie, her family, and her obnoxious
cousin Gerda travel by wagon to the Vida Days celebration where Sadie
enters the sharpshooting contest.
    [1. Sharpshooters—Fiction. 2. Frontier and pioneer life—Fiction.
3. Christian life—Fiction.] I. Title. II. Series: Stahl, Hilda.
Prairie family adventure.
PZ7.S78244Sac 1991   [Fic]—dc20   91-14322
ISBN 0-89107-630-1

99		98		97		96									
15	14	13	12	11	10	9	8	7	6	5	4				

*Dedicated with love
to a special girl
Crystal Fritzler*

Contents

1

Vida Days

The hot Nebraska sun burning down on her, Sadie ducked around the corner of the sod barn and bumped right into Helen, knocking her to the ground. "I'm so sorry!" whispered Sadie as she lifted Helen to her feet and pulled a weed from her baby-fine white braid and brushed off the skirt of her patched calico dress.

Her blue eyes sparkling with the thought of excitement, Helen quickly looked around. "Who're you hidin' from, Sadie?"

"Gerda," whispered Sadie, holding her finger to her lips.

Helen covered her mouth to hide a giggle. "She's a pest. She's our cousin and we are supposed to like her, but she's a real pest."

Sadie frowned at Helen. Momma would not allow them to say that. At eight Helen was the baby

9

of the family, and she got by with things Sadie had never been able to do in all her twelve and a half years. "Don't let Momma hear you say that. You know she's glad to have her Michigan cousins stayin' here."

Helen shrugged her thin shoulders, and her bonnet slipped further down her thin back. "I don't know what's so wrong with sayin' stuff I know you're thinkin' too, Sadie."

Sadie flushed painfully. Sometimes Helen understood too much. Sadie looked off across the vast Nebraska prairie, then back at her little sister. "I'll be glad when they get a place of their own."

"Me too," said Helen. "It is nice to have some-body younger than me here, but I sure get tired of Baby Joey crying all the time. And Gerda thinks she can boss me and Web around." Helen rolled her eyes. "And Gerda sasses! She talks back to Cousin Essie and Cousin Martin!"

Sadie could say a whole lot more about Gerda, but she wouldn't let herself. She was the only one in the family that knew Gerda was really seventeen years old instead of thirteen. Gerda had told her Essie didn't want anyone to know she had a daugh-ter that old.

"I'm glad Gerda's not going to Vida Days with us," said Helen as she swatted away a fly buzzing around her ear.

"Me too," said Sadie.

Vida Days was a three-day celebration in a town northeast of the Circle Y Ranch. It took three hours to drive there in the wagon, and Sadie was so glad she wouldn't have to be in a crowded wagon for three hours with Gerda.

"I asked Daddy if we could please stay all three days," said Helen. "But he said we'll have to come home to do chores. Sadie, don't you ever get tired of doin' chores?"

Sadie nodded.

"When I grow up and get married and have kids, I won't make them do chores!"

"Then they'll be as lazy as Gerda."

Helen gasped. "Then I'll make them work from sunup to sundown like we have to."

Sadie chuckled. Finally she peeked around the corner of the barn. She saw the small sod house Gerda and her parents lived in and the bigger sod house where she lived with Momma and Caleb and Riley, Opal, Web, and Helen. Panting, Tanner lay under Momma's tree, the only tree on the Circle Y Ranch. He lifted his head and whined, then rested his head on his paws again. The Taskers' wagon was parked beside the small sod house. The covered wagon had brought them all the way from Michigan to the edge of the sandhills two months ago. They had planned to stay only a couple of weeks until Mart could find work as a carpenter. He hadn't realized the shortage of lumber in the sandhills, and that meant there were no buildings except sod buildings. Now he had to decide where he could move to make a living for his family.

"Do you see Gerda?" asked Helen, peeking around the barn too.

"I think she went back inside the house with Momma, Essie and Opal," said Sadie. Mart had gone with Caleb, Riley and Web to fix the fence before they all headed for Vida and the great celebration.

"I wish Daddy would hurry back," said Helen. "It's taking all morning just to fix that fence!"

Just then Gerda shouted, "Sadie, come here!"

Sadie pressed against the side of the barn. "Be

11

real quiet, Helen," Sadie whispered. "I don't want her to find me."

"Sadie!" shouted Gerda. "Your momma wants you right now!"

"Momma wants you, Sadie," whispered Helen. "You got to go."

"I know," said Sadie with a long sigh.

"Sadie!" Gerda shouted so loud Sadie was sure the Hepfords could hear it at their place.

"I'm comin'!" shouted Sadie. She took a deep breath, squared her slender shoulders, and walked around the barn with Helen close beside her.

"She looks mad," whispered Helen.

"I know," muttered Sadie.

Tanner ran to Sadie and licked her bare foot and wagged his bushy tail. She rested her hand on his head as she walked toward Gerda. Gerda had her mass of black hair tied back with a yellow ribbon. Her yellow dress and small black shoes looked brand-new. Her blue eyes were flashing with anger.

"I was looking for you, Sadie," snapped Gerda. She ignored Helen.

"I have to see what Momma wants," said Sadie.

"She doesn't really want you," said Gerda smugly. "I only said that so you'd come."

Sadie narrowed her brown eyes.

"That was a mean thing to do," said Helen.

Gerda bent down to Helen and hissed, "Get away! I want to talk to Sadie alone."

Helen flushed, then ran to the house.

Sadie knew Helen wanted to yell at Gerda, but they'd been taught to be kind to others. Sadie lifted her bonnet off her back and tied it in place to hide her face from Gerda. Sadie fingered her brown braids that hung down on her shoulders and stared down at Tanner.

"Well, don't you want to know what I wanted?" asked Gerda sharply.

"What do you want?" asked Sadie tiredly.

"I want to go with your family to town."

Sadie gasped as she shot a look at Gerda. "But why?"

"So I don't have to stay home!"

"But your ma and pa are going. You can't ride with them."

Gerda shook her head. "Joey's sick again, and Ma says they're staying home with him. So I'm going with you, no matter what they say!"

Sadie's heart sank. She knew Gerda always got her own way. "Daddy might not let you ride with us since we have a full wagon."

"If he says that, then I want you to stay home so I can go."

Sadie's eyes widened, and for a minute she couldn't speak. She hadn't been to Jake's Crossing for over a month, and she'd never been to Vida. She'd never agree to stay home.

"If you don't stay home I'll tell everybody you kissed Mitchell Hepford."

"What?" Sadie fell back a step, her face flaming. "Who told you?"

"Gabe."

"How could he? Oh, how could he do such a terrible thing?"

Gerda smiled and shrugged her shoulders. "He likes me and wanted a kiss from me. So I said I'd give him one if he could tell me a secret about you that you wouldn't want anyone to know." Gerda laughed. "So he told me about the kiss."

Blood roared in Sadie's ears. She'd tried to forget about the terrible kiss, but now that Gerda knew, everyone would know!

13

Gerda nudged Sadie in the arm. "If Caleb says there's no room for me in the wagon, you're going to stay home to make room for me." Gerda pushed her face down close to Sadie's. "Or else I'll tell your whole family about the kiss. I'll even tell Levi Cass."

Sadie's legs almost gave way, but she managed to stay standing. "How can you be so mean?"

Gerda giggled. "Am I? I just want to go to Vida Days. It's up to you if I tell or not."

Sadie thought of the horse race, the sharp-shooter contest, and the rodeo she wanted to watch. She'd even daydreamed about entering the sharpshooting contest, but the contestants had to be at Vida Days all three days to enter. "Maybe there'll be room for you," said Sadie weakly.

Gerda shrugged. "Fine. Then nobody has to stay home."

Just then Tanner lifted his head and whined toward the west. Sadie looked across the rolling hills and saw a wagon and a couple of riders coming. It was Caleb on Bay, Riley on Apple, and Mart driving the team with Web in the wagon with him.

"We'll know soon," said Gerda just above a whisper. "Oh, I can't wait to see Levi Cass! He will be in Vida, won't he?"

Sadie wanted to knock Gerda to the ground and yell at her, but she said, "He'll probably be there. Caleb said everybody goes." Caleb had gone each year for the past three years, but this year he said he was more excited about going because he could show off his new family. In April he'd married Momma back in Douglas County, then moved them all to his ranch at the edge of the sandhills. Momma had not known they'd live in a sod house, nor so far away from any neighbors, but she hadn't complained. She loved Caleb so much, it made Sadie blush to watch them look at each other.

"Levi Cass loves me," said Gerda smugly.

Sadie bit back an angry retort because she knew what Gerda said was true. For a while she'd thought about loving Levi when she became old enough to think about such things. Her fifteen-year-old sister Opal thought she loved Levi, and he'd acted like he loved her. But Levi had taken one look at Gerda and had fallen in love with her. Now he barely noticed Opal, and he only talked to Sadie if he wanted something.

"I'm going to spend all the time at Vida Days with Levi," said Gerda.

"Then why did you kiss Gabe Hepford?" asked Sadie as she watched the wagon draw closer.

Gerda laughed breathlessly. "Because I wanted to."

Sadie turned to Gerda in shock. "What about Levi? What would he feel like if he knew?"

Gerda shrugged. "He won't find out." Gerda narrowed her eyes. "And don't you dare tell him!"

"Don't worry! I wouldn't want to hurt him." Sadie turned back to watch the riders and wagon. Riley had ridden on ahead and was almost at the well. At sixteen he was as big as a man, lean and muscled. He was proud of the wide-brimmed hat and slanted high-heeled boots he wore. Until Momma had married Caleb, Riley had been a farmer, but now he was a rancher, and he sat tall and straight in the saddle. He hoped he would never have to walk behind a plow again.

Several minutes later Caleb stopped Bay beside the well, slid to the ground, and waited for Mart to stop Dick and Jane. Caleb stood with his hand resting on the butt of his Colt .45, his booted feet apart. His wide-brimmed hat shielded his eyes and part of his face. He tipped his hat to Gerda and smiled at Sadie. She smiled back. It had taken her a while to love Caleb and call him Daddy, but now she loved him fiercely.

From the wagon beside Mart Web waved at Sadie, and she waved back. Before Sadie could move to help unhitch the team, Gerda ran to Caleb. Sadie saw the flash of impatience cross Caleb's face before he masked it.

Gerda flipped back her mass of black hair. "Caleb, I want to ride to Vida Days with you. Joey is sick again, and Ma's not going."

"What's this about Joey?" asked Mart as he jumped to the ground.

Gerda turned to Mart. "Pa, he's sick again, and Ma says she's going to stay home. I want to go with Caleb and Bess to Vida Days."

Mart took off his cap and scratched his damp blond hair. "If Essie's staying home, I will too."

"What about me?" cried Gerda. "I want to go!" She stamped her foot, and Sadie saw the anger on Caleb's face. He didn't allow that kind of behavior, and he didn't want Mart to either.

Mart patted Gerda's arm. "Now, honey, I'm sure you can ride with Caleb." Mart smiled over Gerda's head at Caleb. "Can you squeeze one more in? You can see the girl has her heart set on going."

"I don't know, Mart. We're pretty crowded."

Sadie held her breath. Would she be forced to stay home?

Mart fingered his cap thoughtfully. "I'll tell you what, Caleb. If you take Gerda with you, I'll do your chores. You can go the full three days. Use my tent and camp out there. Me and Essie will take care of your place."

Sadie's heart leaped with excitement. If Caleb agreed to staying the three whole days at Vida Days, she could enter the sharpshooter contest! Maybe she could win the grand prize, the Winchester Model '76!

2
The Trip

In the wagon Sadie sat as far away from Gerda as she could. Hot wind fluttered the brim of her calico bonnet. The smell of fried rabbit drifted out from the basket beside her. The tent stakes, the folded tent, and the supplies were stacked under the high seat where Caleb and Momma sat. Sadie looked longingly at Riley on Bay. How she wished she could've ridden Apple! Caleb had left her home for Mart.

"It's too hot," said Gerda, fanning her face with the small bit of white cloth she used for a handkerchief while she clutched the side of the wagon to keep from bouncing around. "Tell Riley to let me ride with him!"

Opal rolled her eyes. "You'd get your dress dirty."

Sadie turned away to hide a smile. Opal knew just what to say. Gerda hated to get dirty.

"And you'd get bucked off," said Web with a grin. He loved to tease. He knew Caleb's big bay mare was too well trained to buck anyone off. "You might land right in a fresh cow chip."

"And a rattlesnake would strike you in the face," said Helen with a wicked giggle.

Opal shook her finger at Web and Helen. "Stop that! We don't want anything to ruin our trip." Opal turned away from the kids and gazed out across the rolling hills. Maybe today she'd meet a fine young man to marry next year when she turned sixteen. She thought of Levi Cass and quickly pushed the thoughts aside. She had liked him, but now he had eyes only for Gerda. There were still the Cottonwood Creek bachelors and El and Gabe Hepford. The bachelors were a little old for her, but they were fine-looking men with their own land. They lived in a dugout along the creek. Half the dugout was on Sven Johnson's side and half on Carl White's side. If she married one of them, where would she live? The dugout was too small to share. Maybe all the neighbors would get together and help build them a sod house like they had helped the Hepfords when they'd learned there were no logs to build a log cabin like they'd had in Missouri.

Across the wagon Web turned to Sadie. "I wish I could enter the sharpshooter contest, Sadie."

"Maybe next year you'll be good enough," she said. At nine years Web was almost as big as Sadie. She took after her grandma and was small for her age. Momma said she might always be small. Web was whipcord thin and longed to work alongside Caleb and Riley. "You're already a good shot, Web."

"But not as good as you," said Web with a long sigh.

"Nobody's as good as Sadie," said Helen proudly. "Except maybe Annie Oakley."

"Sadie's not that good," said Gerda, frowning. "I think it's terrible you want to enter that dumb sharpshooter contest. You're a girl!"

Sadie shrugged. "Annie Oakley's a girl too, and she travels all over in the Wild West Show as a sharpshooter."

"Will she be there?" asked Helen, bouncing up and down.

Web jabbed Helen in the ribs. "She won't be there. Vida's not a big town, you know. Not like Omaha."

While Web and Helen talked, Sadie saw a small dot appear on the prairie, then watched it until she could see it was a wagon. Finally she could identify the team pulling the wagon—a cow and a horse. "It's Jewel Comstock!" Sadie cried excitedly. Her best friend Mary Ferguson lived with Jewel near the bachelors on Cottonwood Creek. Sadie lifted her arm high and waved. She saw Mary and Jewel wave back. She heard Malachi bark. The dog stood in the back of the wagon with his great black head hanging over the side.

"I don't like Jewel," said Gerda with a sniff. "She's old, and she wears men's shoes! She has the biggest hooked nose I've ever seen."

Opal frowned at Gerda. "That isn't nice, Gerda. Jewel is our friend."

"Don't tease her team either, Gerda," said Helen. "They don't know they look funny together."

Sadie's heart raced as Jewel drove closer. Sadie blocked out Gerda's constant complaints.

"Howdy, York!" shouted Jewel, her voice loud

enough to be heard up in Dakota Territory. Jewel had known Caleb since he'd first come to Nebraska working as a cowboy for a Texas rancher. He brought the cattle up from Texas to graze on good Nebraska grassland. Caleb had decided to get his own place and build a ranch of his own.

Finally Caleb stopped the team, and Jewel stopped hers. The prairie stretched on as far as the eye could see. Wind blew against the tall grass, making it look like waves of water. The gigantic bright blue sky went on forever until it bent down to touch the waving grass. Far up in the sky an eagle soared. "Howdy, Jewel. Howdy, Mary," said Caleb, tipping his hat.

"Fine weather for Vida Days," said Jewel in her booming voice. Her wagon was loaded down, with room only for Malachi in the back and Mary on the seat.

Sadie wanted to jump from the wagon and run to Mary, but she sat still and smiled at Mary until her face hurt. Mary smiled back. They both knew they couldn't interrupt the adults as they talked about their plans for Vida Days.

"I'm hot!" cried Gerda.

Sadie and the other kids stared at Gerda in shock. How dare she speak when the adults were talking!

Gerda lifted her chin and looked right back at Opal, then Sadie, but she didn't say another word.

Sadie heard Jewel say they were planning to stay the full three days. She'd hired a cowboy to take care of her place while they were gone. Sadie wanted to leap up and shout for joy because she'd have three whole days to spend with Mary, but she sat still and listened.

"You hear about the mail-order bride?" asked

Jewel as she pulled off her limp-brimmed hat that once had been her husband's and rubbed the sweat off her gray hair.

Opal sat up straighter. She wanted to hear about a mail-order bride. She'd considered becoming one if none of the men she knew wanted to marry her next year.

"We never heard a word," said Momma.

"Sven Johnson sent for a mail-order bride from Chicago, Illinois, and plans to meet her and marry her during Vida Days," said Jewel.

"I'll be switched," said Caleb. "What'll Carl White do? Them two bachelors have been together three years already."

Jewel slapped her knee and laughed a great hearty laugh. "I told Carl we could get hitched, but he said he's too old for me."

Sadie giggled. Carl White was in his twenties, and Jewel was over sixty.

"Did Sven build a house?" asked Caleb. The team moved restlessly, and Caleb quieted them with a soft word.

"Never even started one," said Jewel. "I told him more times than you can count he'd better get goin', but he said he had plenty of time. Today he's meeting his bride. Kara Lazlow is her name. Kara Lazlow! From her letters she sounds nice, though perhaps a little timid. Looks pretty enough."

"Looks aren't everything," said Momma. She always said that. "Will she be able to stand the solitude and the hard work?"

Opal smiled dreamily. *She'd* be able to stand the solitude and the hard work. She'd make a good bride for a fine young man.

Sadie twisted her bonnet string around her finger. She wouldn't want to be a mail-order bride.

It would be scary to marry someone you didn't know. Someday she'd marry a man just like Caleb York.

"You heard about the sharpshooter?" asked Jewel.

"No," said Caleb.

Sadie's stomach knotted, and she held her breath.

"Red Colvin," said Jewel as if she'd said Buffalo Bill Cody himself.

"I heard of him," said Caleb. "Never met him, though."

"He's known from here to Texas for his marksmanship," said Jewel. "He'll be entering the sharpshooter contest. Big redheaded fellow with an ugly scar on his right cheek. He likes to win."

Sadie's heart sank. She'd thought she had a chance to win the Winchester '76. If Red Colvin was as good as Jewel said, she wouldn't stand a chance. Maybe she shouldn't even try.

"I best get," said Jewel. "I told Barkers we'd stop by and lend a hand so they could go to Vida Days."

Mary waved at Sadie, and Sadie waved back as Caleb called to Dick and Jane to get up.

"Are you scared, Sadie?" asked Helen, bumping against Sadie as the wagon moved.

"About what?" asked Sadie even though she knew what.

"Red Colvin," said Helen.

Web stuck out his chest and wrapped his fingers around his suspenders. "I wouldn't be!"

"I would," said Helen with a shiver. "I bet he can shoot the eye out of a fly. Sadie, you can only shoot the wings off."

Gerda laughed and rolled her eyes. "Sadie

24

York, you don't really think you can enter a sharp-shooter contest, do you? Everybody will laugh at you . . . Especially me and Levi."

"*We* won't laugh," snapped Helen, frowning at Gerda. Helen turned to Web. "We won't laugh, will we?"

Web shook his head. How he wished he was good enough to enter. He'd shoot against Red Colvin and be proud doing it!

Sadie turned her face into the hot wind and tried to ignore the butterflies fluttering in her stomach.

3
Camp

Sadie watched Web and Helen race around the tent she'd helped Caleb and Riley set up. Momma and the girls were to sleep in the tent and Caleb and the boys under the wagon. Sadie glanced at Gerda. She was frowning down at dust on her yellow dress. Momma and Opal were making a campfire to cook supper.

Other wagons and tents were scattered across the outskirts of Vida. Music drifted out from a big barn near the livery. People swarmed around, laughing and talking. Smells of manure, campfires, and cooking food mixed together to create an odor Sadie didn't like. The sound of fiddle music suddenly covered all other sounds. "Mitch?" muttered Sadie. He played the fiddle, but then so did a lot of other people. She looked around for Mitch Hepford, but couldn't see him. She frowned. When she found

27

him, she'd tell him how angry she was that Gabe told Gerda about the kiss. Mitch would probably throw back his head and laugh.

Sadie looked toward the makeshift corral, but didn't see the Hepfords' mule. She saw people standing in the shade of two giant cottonwoods that stood at the side of a creek. The Hepfords weren't there. She'd find Mitch, though, and she'd box his ears. She frowned, then sighed heavily. Jesus didn't want her to box Mitch's ears, even if he deserved it. She sighed again. Jesus didn't want her to be angry at Mitch either.

Just then Web slid to a stop in front of Sadie. "I'm gonna look for Red Colvin just to see what he looks like. Daddy said we could look around. Want to come?"

Helen tugged on Sadie's hand. "Come on, Sadie. We'll look at him and see what his scar looks like. I never saw a scar on a face before. I wonder how he got that scar."

Sadie shook her finger at Helen. "Don't you dare stare at his scar, and don't ask him about it! I mean it, Helen Irene Merrill York!"

Helen grinned and flipped her braid over her thin shoulder. "I might ask and I might not!"

Sadie groaned and shook her head.

"Let's go look for Red Colvin," said Web.

"All right," said Sadie. She did want to get a look at him. Maybe he wouldn't come after all, and then she'd enter the sharpshooter contest for sure.

"Where're you going?" asked Gerda, running after them.

"Oh no," said Helen. She dropped Sadie's hand and raced after Web. She looked over her shoulder at Sadie. "I might even ask to touch his scar," she called, then giggled.

Sadie clicked her tongue. Momma and Caleb would have to stop spoiling Helen. Sadie looked longingly after Web and Helen as they ran toward Vida, but she waited for Gerda.

"Where're you going?" Gerda asked again.

"To look around," Sadie said with a shrug.

"I'll go with you," said Gerda, laughing. "Maybe we'll find Levi Cass."

Sadie clamped her lips tightly. She would not yell at Gerda!

Suddenly a riderless horse galloped toward them, its reins bouncing up and down. Sadie jumped aside, but Gerda stood rooted to the spot, too afraid to move. With a cry Sadie leaped toward Gerda, grabbed her by the arm, and jerked her out of the way just as the horse galloped past, sending sand spraying from its hooves. Sweat popped out on Sadie's face, and her legs almost gave way. She watched a man leap forward, grab the reins, and stop the horse.

"You girls all right?" the man called.

Sadie nodded and tried to stop trembling.

"You saved my life," whispered Gerda, staring at Sadie in surprise. "You could've been killed!"

Sadie shrugged. "I didn't think what I was doing . . . I just did it."

"Well, I wouldn't have!"

Sadie smiled weakly. Gerda was probably right. "Remember how you saved Levi's life a couple of months ago when those men were going to hang him because they thought he was a horse thief?"

Gerda smiled and lifted her head proudly. "I did, didn't I?" She smoothed down her dress and retied her bonnet. "Let's walk around and see if we can find Levi."

Sadie fell into step with Gerda, and they walked down the path already worn in the grass by the people who had camped out for Vida Days. Vida was larger than Jake's Crossing. Some of the buildings were made of wood and others of sod. A banner strung across the dirt street fluttered in the wind. Bold red lettering said, *WELCOME TO VIDA DAYS!* The wooden sidewalks were crowded with people. Horses and wagons lined the dusty streets. The noise buzzed inside Sadie's head, and she longed for the great silence of the prairie.

"Isn't it grand!" cried Gerda, looking around and smiling happily. "I'm going to tell Pa to move to Vida. He could find work here." She stopped at a window full of women's hats. "Sadie, look! I want a hat just like that one." She pointed to a big hat full of feathers and flowers. "Oh, the feathers are beautiful!"

Sadie wrinkled her nose. The hat was pretty, but she'd never wear such a creation. It was a hat for a town woman, not a hard-working country woman. Momma would never wear such a hat either. Sadie thought of the wide-brimmed black hat Levi had given her from the peddler's wagon, and she smiled. She loved her black hat, and she'd have it on right now except Momma had told her to wear her bonnet like a proper lady. But she would wear the hat when she shot in the contest.

Suddenly Gerda grabbed Sadie's arm. "Look at all those men!"

Sadie looked across the street where several men Riley's age and older were standing and talking. "They're cowboys," said Sadie.

"I'm going to talk to them," said Gerda, her face flushed and her eyes sparkling.

Sadie gasped and caught at Gerda's arm. "No!

30

You're not a saloon girl! You can't just walk up to strange men and talk to them!"

Gerda lifted her chin. "I'm going to anyway. You stay here and wait for me."

"I won't!" Sadie shook her head hard. "I'll go find Web and Helen and walk around with them."

"Oh, all right! Do what you want, but I'm going to have some fun." Gerda stepped off the sidewalk, waited for a wagon to pass, then crossed the street.

Sadie's cheeks burned with embarrassment for Gerda. "I wish Opal was here. She'd know what to do." Sadie slowly walked away, her head down. Suddenly she bumped into someone. Startled, she looked up to see a dark-haired girl her age glaring at her. Another girl stood beside her and two boys behind them. "Sorry," mumbled Sadie.

"Country girl!" snapped the dark-haired girl. "No manners."

"Melinda, don't blame her," said a small blonde girl. "She doesn't have time to learn how to act like a lady."

Sadie flushed painfully. The girls and boys were dressed in nice clothes. The girls had giant white bows tied to their braids. The boys wore white shirts. Sadie could tell they were town kids.

"I see you don't know how to talk either," said Melinda with a sneer.

One of the boys stepped forward and smiled at Sadie. "I'm Jake, and this is Miles. The girls are Melinda and Grace. What's your name?"

Sadie hesitated. "Sadie York," she said just above a whisper.

"Sadie York!" they all said together, then laughed.

Sadie felt on fire. The patches on her calico dress and black leather shoes suddenly seemed to stand out boldly. She tried to push past the kids, but Miles blocked her way. He was shorter than Riley, but still much taller than Sadie.

"Tell us about yourself, Sadie," said Jake as he pushed his cap back on his light brown hair. His blue eyes twinkled mischievously. "Do you have a family? Or were you hatched by a prairie chicken?"

The others laughed harder, and Sadie wanted to run and hide. Suddenly Sadie thought of the dangers she'd faced and lived to tell about. She could face these town kids without fear, couldn't she?

She lifted her chin, and sparks flew from her eyes. "Please let me pass! I don't want to cause trouble, but I will if you don't stop tormenting me."

"Oh, ho! A feisty little country bumpkin!" Miles poked Sadie's arm. "Country bumpkin!"

Sadie bit back an angry retort and once again tried to push past the kids. Jake caught her arm and brought her up short. He untied her bonnet and lifted it off her head.

"Got any fleas in there?" Jake asked, thumping her head as they all laughed.

Suddenly Sadie pushed hard against Jake's chest, hooked her foot around his leg near his ankle, and jerked. Jake fell backwards to the dusty street. She turned on the others while Jake jumped up swearing. "Leave me alone! . . . All of you!" Sadie walked away, her cheeks bright red and her body damp with sweat. How glad she was Opal hadn't seen what she'd done! Opal would've shamed her on the spot for acting unladylike. And Opal would've told Momma. Sadie walked faster. If Momma knew, she might take out the special spanking board she'd brought in the wagon with her and spank her even though she was twelve and a half years old.

Just as Sadie started past the hardware store she saw a sign that said, *SHARPSHOOTERS SIGN UP HERE.* Her heart almost exploded inside her. Should she put her name there? Yes! Yes, she'd sign up and she'd win the Winchester '76!

Blood pounding in her ears, Sadie walked into the crowded store. She eased her way past several women chattering about their gardens and stopped at the counter where she was to sign up. She picked up the short stub of a pencil and bent over the ledger that held a list of names.

"That's only for the sharpshooters, little lady," said the man behind the counter.

Flushing painfully, Sadie looked up. "I know."

The man laughed good-naturedly. "Then go ahead and sign. It'll be two bits."

Sadie froze. Two bits! Where would she get twenty-five cents? "I didn't know it cost to enter," she said weakly.

"I'll pay the two bits," said a man behind Sadie.

She whirled around and stared up at a tall red-headed man about Caleb's age. He wore a leather vest over a striped shirt and dark pants with a gun-belt low on his hip. He had a white scar on his right cheek. It was Red Colvin!

He smiled and doffed his black wide-brimmed hat. "I'd be honored to pay for the little mite's entry fee," said Red with a grin.

Sadie swallowed hard. "No, thank you. I'll pay my own."

"What's your name, little mite?" asked Red.

"Sadie York."

Red dropped some money on the counter.

"This is for Sadie York and for me." He smiled wider at Sadie. "I'm Red Colvin. Call me Red."

Sadie smiled, suddenly feeling better. "My momma wouldn't want me to take money from you."

"You didn't." Red jabbed his thumb at the man behind the counter. "He did." Red looped his thumbs in his gunbelt. "We'll make a swap here, little mite. I'll pay your two bits if you sign us both up. I want folks to be able to read my name in the ledger." He bent down to Sadie. "You can read and write, can't you?"

"Yes."

"Thought so. You look bright. And you must be able to shoot since you're aimin' to sign up."

"I can shoot," said Sadie, smiling. "I hear you can too."

"Some," he said.

The man behind the counter laughed. "Some! You're the champion, and everybody knows it."

"Maybe not this year," said Red, winking at Sadie.

She grinned, then turned and in her careful hand wrote her name, then Red Colvin's right under it. Web and Helen would love hearing about this!

"I'll see you at the shooting range later, Sadie York," said Red.

"I'll see you, Red Colvin." Sadie smiled, then walked toward the open door of the store. Just then she saw the town kids on the sidewalk outside the store. She stopped, her heart racing. Would they all jump her at once?

"Trouble, little mite?" asked Red from behind Sadie.

She turned slowly, her cheeks red with embarrassment. "I'm not scared of those kids outside."

"I don't reckon you are."

"They were pickin' on me, and I knocked the big boy down."

Red chuckled. "I'll walk you out. I got business at the stage stop anyhow." Red tugged his hat lower on his forehead and strode toward the door. He stepped aside at the open door and motioned for Sadie to precede him. "After you," he said politely.

Sadie squared her shoulders, lifted her chin, and walked out. The town kids backed away and let her pass.

Red chuckled. "A reputation helps keep those rascals in hand."

"They don't much care for country kids," said Sadie.

Red winked at Sadie. "They might not, but I do. I was born and raised in Illinois, then took up repairin' guns and on the way became known as a sharpshooter." He stopped outside the stage stop. "I got gear comin' in on the stage." He motioned up the street at a cloud of dust. "Here it comes now."

Sadie backed up against the building to get away from the dust. Harnesses rattled on the four mules pulling the stage. The driver shouted and pulled back on the reins. Dust billowed out, then finally settled. Sadie watched as a man opened the stage door to let out the passengers. Two men and a woman stepped out.

Sadie looked closer at the woman. She seemed frightened, and she didn't look much older than Opal as she glanced around as if she were expecting someone. She had light brown hair with a tiny hat perched on it and wide blue eyes. She was not much taller than Sadie.

"Excuse me, please," the woman said to the man who was unloading the stage. "I'm looking for Sven Johnson."

Sadie gasped. The woman was Sven's mail-order bride!

4

The Mail-order Bride

Sadie stepped forward. "Kara Lazlow?"

The woman's face lit up. "Yes, I'm Kara Lazlow."

"I'm Sadie York. I know Sven Johnson. He's not here right now, but you can go back to camp with me to wait for him."

Kara bit her bottom lip and gripped the strings of her handbag tightly. "I don't know if I should leave here. He said he'd meet me."

Sadie smiled. She felt sorry for Kara. "I'll wait with you. If he doesn't come before long, we'll leave word here and go to camp. You'll like my sister Opal. She's fifteen."

"I'm seventeen." Kara gasped, then slapped her gloved hand over her mouth. "Please, please, don't tell! Sven thinks I'm nineteen." Kara patted her flushed cheeks with her fingertips. "I didn't mean to lie. It just happened. After he answered my letter and said he was looking for a woman between nineteen and twenty-five, I decided I'd better tell him I was nineteen." Kara's voice faded away.

Sadie sighed. First Gerda, now Kara!

"There's my trunk," said Kara as the man dropped it on the wooden sidewalk near other luggage.

Sadie wondered how they'd ever get the trunk to the camp by themselves. She looked around for Red Colvin to ask for his help, but he wasn't in sight.

Kara swayed slightly, then eased herself down on her trunk. "I didn't get much rest nor much to eat since I left Chicago . . . And it's very hot." She dabbed perspiration from her face with a small hanky she pulled from the sleeve of her gray traveling suit.

"I could get you a bite to eat, but I don't have any money, so we'll have to wait until we're in camp."

Kara started to open her handbag, then studied Sadie thoughtfully. "Do you really know Sven?"

"Yes. Most Sundays he and Carl White come to our house for singin' and preachin'."

"Who's your father?"

"Caleb York."

Kara's face brightened. "From Texas?"

Sadie nodded.

"Sven mentioned him in his letters. He said Caleb York had children, but I thought he meant little ones."

"He didn't."

"Then you know what my house looks like, don't you? Is it big or little? Are there pretty curtains on the windows?"

Sadie moved from one foot to the other. The bachelors lived in a dugout along the creek bank. But how could she tell that to Kara? "Wait and ask Sven," Sadie finally said.

Tears welled up in Kara's blue eyes. "Why didn't he come to meet me? Do you think he changed his mind?"

"I don't think so." Sadie told Kara about meeting Jewel Comstock earlier and what she'd said.

Kara slowly stood and dabbed at her eyes. "It doesn't do any good to sit here and feel sorry for myself. I'll go with you. We can get my trunk later."

Sadie watched as Kara talked to the station manager about her trunk. Kara seemed very capable even though she was small and from the city.

Kara caught Sadie's hand and squeezed it. "Tell me about yourself. Why are you here now?"

Sadie told Kara about Vida Days as they walked slowly down the sidewalk. Near the barbershop they walked around a noisy crowd. Sadie told Kara about the sharpshooter contest, and Kara laughed and stopped right in the middle of the sidewalk, her cheeks flushed rosy red and her eyes sparkling.

"I want to enter it, Sadie! Where do I register?"

Sadie could hardly believe her ears. Maybe Kara wasn't such a city girl after all. "In the hardware store. It costs two bits."

"I don't care!" Kara gripped Sadie's arm. "Don't tell Sven. He might object like Papa always did."

"Did your papa object to you coming west to the sandhills?"

Kara's jaw tightened. "Yes, but I don't want to discuss it."

Sadie shrugged. It didn't matter to her, but she knew Gerda would want to know every detail about

39

Kara. At thoughts of Gerda, Sadie glanced quickly around as they walked. Where was Gerda? Had she returned to camp?

A few minutes later Sadie and Kara walked into the crowded hardware store. It smelled of sweat and gun oil. "Sign your name here, Kara."

Kara signed her name with a flourish, then paid the twenty-five cents. She read the sign posted beside the ledger that gave the times of the contest each day. "The contest starts in two hours. Is the contest field far from here?"

"No. It's near where we camped, just outside of Vida." Sadie walked back outdoors with Kara. "Come meet my family. You'll like my sister Opal."

"Will I?"

"She works hard at being a lady."

"Will she be shooting in the contest?"

Sadie laughed as they waited for two buggies to drive past before they crossed the street. "No. She can shoot, but she's not very accurate. But she cooks and sews real good."

Just then Sadie heard a scream that sounded just like Gerda's. Sadie's stomach knotted. What trouble was Gerda in this time? Sadie looked quickly around. How she wanted to ignore the scream, but she knew she couldn't. Sadie turned to Kara. "Wait here for me. I think my cousin's in trouble."

Sadie raced along the side of the feed store to the sound of another scream. At the back of the building she saw Gerda struggling to get away from a fat man with a balding head. He was trying to kiss Gerda, and she screamed again. Sadie ran to the man and kicked him in the leg. "Let her go right now!"

The man swore as he turned his head toward

Sadie. But he didn't release his hold on Gerda. "Get away from here, kid."

"Help me, Sadie!" cried Gerda, struggling hard. Her yellow dress was wrinkled and dusty, and her bonnet had slipped off her head.

"You get out of here, kid!" snapped the man with an angry scowl. Red scratches ran down his left cheek. His hat lay on the ground, and sweat soaked the front of his dark blue shirt.

Just then Kara walked around Sadie, taking her hat off as she did. She held a long hat pin between her fingers and said softly, "Turn the girl loose right now!"

Gerda stopped struggling and stared at Kara.

"I'm gettin' real mad, girls," said the man as he tightened his hold on Gerda. "Both of you mind your own business."

Kara stepped up to the man, jabbed her hat pin in the man's rear end, and pulled it back out.

Sadie gasped in surprise.

With a shriek of pain the man turned Gerda free and grabbed his backside. He swore roundly, burning Sadie's ears.

Gerda dashed to Sadie and clung to her arm. "He jumped right out and grabbed me! He wouldn't let me go!"

"Let's get out of here, girls," said Kara as she calmly pinned her hat back in place.

Sadie and Gerda ran back to the sidewalk, with Kara close on their heels. Sadie glanced back to see the man running toward them, but when he saw the crowd on the sidewalk he ducked his head and turned the other way.

"That man was awful to me!" cried Gerda, blinking tears from her eyes.

"You should not be on the streets on your own," said Kara.

Gerda glared at Kara. "Are you my mother?"

"No, but I'm smart enough to know to stay where I belong," said Kara.

Sadie quickly introduced the two.

"A mail-order bride!" cried Gerda with a laugh. "I expected an ugly old maid. What's wrong with you? Why would you be forced to find a man through the mail?"

Kara lifted her chin. "I would rather not say."

Sadie hid a smile. She knew that answer was like waving a red flag at a bull. Gerda would do everything she could to learn why Kara had become a mail-order bride. At least the mystery seemed to take Gerda's mind off her attacker.

Back at camp Momma and Opal were delighted to meet Kara. Opal led Kara into the tent to rest with the understanding that Sadie would return in time to get her for the shooting contest.

"Sadie, ask Caleb to get Kara's trunk for her," said Momma. "He's near the corral talking with Zane Hepford."

Sadie shot a look at Gerda, willing her to keep her mouth shut.

"Where is Mitch?" asked Gerda innocently.

Sadie wished she'd left Gerda in the hands of the terrible man.

Momma pushed back a damp strand of graying hair. "He was here a while ago looking for Sadie."

Gerda giggled and ducked into the tent.

Sadie flushed as she walked toward the corral to find Caleb. What would she do if Gerda decided to tell about the kiss?

Just before Sadie reached the corral Web and

Helen ran up to her, looking ready to burst with excitement. They were dusty and damp with sweat.

"We found him, Sadie," said Helen, bobbing up and down, sending her braids bouncing.

"We found Red Colvin," said Web. "He's mean."

Sadie stopped short. "Why do you say that?"

"We saw him beat a man up," said Web, jabbing the air with his fists.

"And he yelled at us when he saw us watching," said Helen. She wrinkled her nose. "I never got to ask him about his scar."

Sadie frowned thoughtfully. Red had been nice to her. Maybe he'd had good reason to beat the man up. She didn't have time to sort it out now, so she pushed the thoughts to the back of her mind. "I have to talk to Daddy," she said.

"He's on the way to watch the footrace," said Web.

Sadie gasped. "But I was going to enter! Where's it held?"

"Just over there," said Helen, pointing to the far side of the corral.

Sadie ran to the marked area. About fifty people were standing on the sidelines to watch. Suddenly butterflies fluttered in her stomach. Could she run with so many people watching?

"There's Daddy," said Web, pointing toward a group of men.

Sadie dashed to Caleb's side, but didn't speak until the short, bald man who was talking finished what he was saying. "I need to talk to you, Daddy," Sadie whispered.

"What is it, Sadie Rose?" asked Caleb in his soft Texas drawl. He always called her Sadie Rose no matter how often she told him she was only called Sadie. He smiled down at Sadie as the men

43

drifted away, deep in conversation. "Why aren't you in line for the race?"

"I'm going, but I had to tell you to please pick up Kara Lazlow's trunk at the stage stop." Sadie quickly told about meeting Kara. "She's in the tent with Momma and Opal."

"I'll go right after the footrace and before the shooting match," said Caleb, tugging Sadie's braid. "I wouldn't want to miss either."

Sadie smiled as her heart swelled with love. Nobody had a better pa than they did!

"You did sign up, didn't you?"

Sadie nodded. "I might not shoot in the contest. Not with the sharpshooter Red Colvin shooting."

"God is with you, Sadie Rose. You can do all things through Christ who strengthens you. That includes a footrace and a shooting contest."

"Thanks, Daddy."

"You're my special Sadie Rose."

Sadie smiled as she ran to the starting line. Suddenly she stopped short. Mitch and Good One stood side by side with about six others. She'd run races with both Mitch and Good One before. At times she'd beat Mitch, but she'd never been able to beat the Pawnee warrior.

They both smiled at her. Was Mitch looking smug? Would he convince Gerda to spread the story about the kiss?

Sadie stepped back a step, her hands locked together in front of her and her eyes glued to Mitch Hepford.

44

5
The Footrace

"I won't race," muttered Sadie, taking another step back.

"Sadie York!" called Mitch Hepford, waving. Hot wind ruffled his dark hair. His black eyes gleamed with mischief. "It's almost time for the race to begin!"

Good One lifted his hand and smiled at Sadie. He wore a blue shirt, dark pants, and high-topped moccasins. "Come race, Fleet Foot," he said. He'd called her that since the first time she'd raced him. But that had been for her life and not a contest. Since then they'd become friends.

Sadie sighed heavily. It would look strange if she didn't race. She ran to get in line. Blood tingled in her veins. How she loved to run! She smiled at Good One and said, "Hi." She couldn't look at Mitch.

"What's wrong with you, Sadie?" asked Mitch in a low voice.

Slowly Sadie turned to him. Her mouth felt bone-dry. Before she could speak, the announcer called for them to get ready. Sadie leaned down, her eyes on the red flag across the prairie. She knew they had to run to the line, then back. The first one back would win a pair of boots. Mitch had told her several days ago that he wanted the boots. He'd always admired Riley's. Mitch's pa said they didn't have enough cash money to spend on boots, so Mitch was determined to win them.

Suddenly the starting gun cracked. Sadie leaped forward, her eyes on the red flag. She flew across the dried grass, her feet barely touching the ground. Wind blew her bonnet off her head, and it flopped to her back. She heard the shouts from the line of people watching. Twice she heard her own name called, and that made her run faster.

She reached the line where the red flag stood, then turned and sped back the way she'd come. She heard the other runners, and up ahead she saw Good One. She knew if she turned her head she'd see Mitch beside her. But she didn't turn her head or she'd lose stride. She forced more speed until her ears roared and her lungs almost burst. Sweat popped out on her face, and the wind dried it.

Suddenly Good One stumbled, then sprawled to the ground. His horn of black hair flopped over his otherwise bald head. Sadie's heart dropped to her feet. Was he hurt?

Sadie sped past Good One. Now she had a chance to win! She'd beat Mitch, and he'd never get to own a pair of boots! A cold band tightened around her heart. What if Good One was hurt? If he'd jumped up, he'd have passed her by now. She slowed, and Mitch sped past. She hesitated, turned, and ran back to Good One. She dropped down beside him, her chest heaving. He groaned, but didn't move. "Are you hurt?" she asked in alarm.

"You lost race," Good One said as he weakly pushed himself up.

"What happened to you?" she asked as she helped him stand.

"A great pain hit me here." He touched his chest. His bronze skin looked ashen. "The years on the reservation took away my health."

"Will you be all right?" asked Sadie in concern.

Good One nodded. He looked over Sadie's head as the crowd roared. "Race is over," he said. "Mitch won."

"I don't mind," said Sadie. "I just want to make sure you're all right."

"You are full of kindness, Fleet Foot."

Sadie smiled, pleased at his kind words. "Not always."

"I will go home before more pain hits," said Good One.

"Did you come with Joshua and Lost Sand Cherry?" Lost Sand Cherry was Good One's sister and was married to Joshua Cass. Until just a few weeks ago Levi Cass had been embarrassed to let anyone know his stepmother was a Pawnee Indian.

Good One shook his head. "I drove my peddler wagon."

"I'll walk you to it," said Sadie. She saw Mitch receive the fancy cowboy boots for winning the race, and for a minute she wished they were hers, but pushed the thought aside. She had wanted to

47

help Good One. He was more important than a pair of cowboy boots.

Several minutes later Sadie watched Good One drive the bright red and yellow peddler's wagon away.

"You're nice, Sadie York," Mitch said from behind her. "You could've won the race."

Sadie hesitated, then spun around. "Why did you tell about . . . about the . . . kiss?" The last word almost choked her. She'd kissed him so he'd give her a box of paper, something she'd wanted more than anything else. She knew she'd been wrong to do it, but it was over and done and she had to forgive herself for doing such a terrible thing.

Mitch shot a look around, then scowled at Sadie as he wrapped his hands around his suspenders. The cowboy boots were on his feet. "Somebody might hear you," he whispered gruffly.

Sadie stepped closer to Mitch. She smelled sweat and dust on him. "Gabe told Gerda!"

Mitch looked as if he'd been kicked by his pa's mule. "This is the worst thing that's ever happened to me! What if Pa finds out? He'd skin me alive!"

"I hope nobody else finds out!"

"Gerda's tongue wags all the time. She might tell," said Mitch with his shoulders drooping and his head down.

"She'd better not," said Sadie grimly.

"I wish your cousin was as nice as you," said Mitch.

Sadie blushed.

"Gabe thinks she'd make a good wife. He's eighteen, and he said if she was old enough he'd marry her."

Sadie's eyes lit up. Gerda *was* old enough! It

would serve her right to marry into the all-male Hepford family!

"I'll be glad when Gabe or El gets married so I can quit cookin'." Mitch chuckled. "I think I'll tell Gabe Gerda wants to marry him."

"Mitch, you can't lie!"

Mitch chuckled.

Just then Sadie heard Mary calling to her.

"I don't never want Mary to find out about the kiss," said Mitch in agony.

Sadie looked at him in shock. "I thought you hated Mary."

Mitch flushed. "I don't no more. I was over at Jewel's, and me and Mary hayed together. We get along fine now."

Sadie stared at Mitch in shock, then turned as Mary ran up. Mary's copper-brown hair glistened in the sunlight, and her blue eyes sparkled.

"Hello, Sadie," said Mary in her English accent. Her blue gingham dress looked almost new. Her cheeks turned pink as she smiled at Mitch. "Hello, Mitch."

"Hi, Mary," said Mitch softly.

Sadie started to say something to Mary, then saw how she was looking at Mitch. Sadie's heart sank. Had she lost her best friend?

Mary flushed and turned back to Sadie, then hugged her tightly. "I was afraid we wouldn't make it until dark! What shall we do now?"

"We could walk around town," said Sadie. Then she remembered the shooting contest. "I'm sorry, Mary, but it's time for me to get my rifle and go shoot."

Mary's eyes widened. "Are you really going to shoot with Red Colvin shooting too?"

"Yes," said Sadie as her stomach once again knotted painfully.

"I heard about Red Colvin," said Mitch. "Sadie, you're no match for him."

Sadie's heart sank.

Mary shook her finger at Mitch. "Stop that! Sadie is a good shot! She just might win!"

Mitch grinned. "We can watch her together. If she wins I'll buy you an ice cream, Mary."

Flushing, Mary laughed. "What happens if she loses?"

"I'll still buy you an ice cream."

Sadie frowned at them. "I'll see you later." She forced back thoughts of Mitch and Mary as she ran to the tent to get Kara.

Opal stepped out of the tent just as Sadie arrived. Opal's long nutmeg-brown hair hung down her back and spread out over her green gingham dress. "Sadie, Daddy told us you lost the race because you helped Good One. That was nice of you." Opal prided herself on being kind, but she didn't know if she could ever be nice enough to help someone if it meant losing something she wanted badly.

Sadie shrugged. She didn't want to talk about the race. "I came to get Kara for the shooting contest."

"She's sound asleep," said Opal, glancing back at the tent.

"I'll wake her up."

Opal caught Sadie's arm. "She was very tired, Sadie. Let her sleep."

Sadie shook her head. "She wants to shoot."

Opal couldn't understand why Sadie or Kara would want to shoot in the contest against all the men.

"Did Sven Johnson stop by yet?" Sadie asked.

Opal shook her head. "Don't you think that's odd?"

Sadie nodded.

"He made arrangements to meet her at the stage stop. They're going to get married tomorrow or the next day."

Sadie didn't want to sort it all out. "Ask Caleb about it," said Sadie as she ducked through the tent flap. It was breathlessly hot inside the tent, and Sadie didn't know how Kara could sleep. Sadie bent down and shook Kara's shoulder gently. Kara jumped, and her eyes flew open. "Time to go shoot," said Sadie.

Kara jumped up, shook her skirts in place, carefully smoothed back the strands of light brown hair that had escaped the bun, then pinned her hat back in place. "I'm ready."

Outside the tent Sadie lifted her rifle from the back of the wagon. "Opal, are you going to watch?"

Opal hesitated, then nodded. A shooting match would be a good place to see what fine young men were available.

"Where's Gerda?" asked Sadie with a quick look around.

"With Momma," said Opal, rolling her eyes.

Kara touched the stock on Sadie's rifle. "Can I use your rifle in the contest?"

"Sure. But you'll have to shoot a couple of times to get the feel of it."

"I'm sure they'll give me a chance to." Kara suddenly laughed. "I hope Sven Johnson doesn't come get me today!"

Sadie and Opal exchanged puzzled looks, then walked with Kara to the open prairie where they'd set up a firing range. Several fence posts were lined up with paper targets on them. The bull's-eye looked so big that Sadie knew she wouldn't have any trouble shooting all three shots into it. She looked at the line of contestants. They were all men. She saw several men she didn't know, as well as Caleb, Riley, Joshua and Levi Cass, Red Colvin, and the two bachelors from Cottonwood Creek. She darted a look at Kara. She was looking at Red Colvin as if she'd seen a ghost. She didn't even notice Sven Johnson.

"I must speak to someone," whispered Kara, her face white.

Before Sadie could follow her, the town kids ran up, laughing and jeering.

"You can't really shoot that big gun, can you?" asked Jake, jabbing Sadie's shoulder.

Sadie tried to walk past them without saying anything, but they circled her and wouldn't let her pass. "Be careful! This gun is loaded," she said sharply.

"Do you really think you're going to enter the sharpshooting contest?" asked Melinda, laughing wickedly.

Sadie's face burned. Somehow she had to get away from the terrible town kids. Why wouldn't they leave her alone? Helplessly she looked toward the line of contenders. None of them looked her way. Kara was deep in conversation with Red Colvin. Sven Johnson didn't seem to notice her.

"Let's take her gun," said a dark-haired boy Sadie hadn't seen before.

Sadie gripped her rifle and faced the boy squarely. "Get out of my way . . . Now!" Her voice rang out with authority, and to her surprise the town kids backed away and let her through. She walked toward Caleb, her head high and her rifle at her side. Her heart hammered as she listened for sounds of the town kids behind her.

6

Ten Sharpshooters

Her heart racing, Sadie stopped at Caleb's side. He smiled at her, and she immediately felt better. He'd protect her from the town kids if they tried anything.

"Are you all set, Sadie Rose?" asked Caleb softly.

She nodded as she glanced around at the noisy onlookers and the silent shooters. She saw Sven Johnson glance toward Kara, then look away as if he didn't know her. Didn't he recognize his own mail-order bride? Sadie watched Red and Kara talking intently together, then scowl at each other. He turned his back on her, and she lifted her chin, squared her shoulders and walked to Sadie's side.

"Do you know Red Colvin, Kara?" asked Sadie in surprise.

She nodded and looked very grim, so Sadie didn't press the issue.

Sadie looked at Red Colvin again just as another man strode to the group. Red and the man spotted each other, and Sadie could feel the angry tension between them. Who was the tall bearded man with the big silver buckle on his belt?

"Could I see your rifle, Sadie?" asked Kara, reaching for the gun.

Sadie handed it to her, and Kara lifted it to her shoulder and looked down the barrel. Finally she handed it back.

"I won't have any trouble shooting it," Kara said. "Thanks."

Sadie nodded, then glanced around to see where Levi and Joshua Cass were. She saw them with other men waiting to shoot. Levi looked her way, smiled slightly, then turned back. Maybe Levi was embarrassed to know her. Many people thought she was making a spectacle of herself by entering the contest. She knew they thought the same of Kara. Sadie squared her shoulders and looked straight ahead.

Just then a big man with thinning gray hair stepped to the front of the shooters. He lifted his hand for silence. "Good evening, ladies and gentlemen." He glanced at Sadie and Kara and blinked in surprise, then quickly caught himself. "I'm Taylor Jennings, mayor of Vida, for those who don't know me. I want to welcome all of you today and wish you all good luck." He glanced down the line of shooters. "This is a three-day event. Today we pick the ten best shooters, tomorrow the five best, and the last day of Vida Days we'll see who is the champion sharpshooter and the winner of the Winchester '76." Everyone clapped and cheered. When they were silent again, he said, "Each of you gets three shots each day. Each of you has a number. The scorekeeper is Davis Greavy down by the targets. Give him a hand, and welcome all the shooters."

Sadie's stomach tightened as everyone clapped and shouted and whistled. The sounds rolled out over the prairie and were lost among the hills.

Taylor Jennings looked right at Sadie and Kara. "We'd ordinarily say ladies first, but since we're going by the numbers, we can't. Will the first five shooters get on your marks."

Sadie's number was six and Kara's was eleven. Sadie watched as the first five men took aim and fired. Only one of the shooters hit the bull's-eye with all three shots. He was the tall bearded man with a big silver buckle on his belt, the man Red Colvin didn't like. Taylor Jennings called him Quint Largo. Sadie saw another look of anger pass between Red Colvin and Quint Largo.

Sadie's mouth felt cotton-dry, and she longed for a drink of icy cold well water.

"Next row!" called Taylor Jennings.

Sadie trembled, but stepped forward. She watched Davis Greavy change the targets. Sadie took a deep breath. She knew with the Lord helping her she could shoot her very best. Just then she heard the town kids calling her name in a taunting manner. Her muscles tightened. She knew if she didn't relax she'd miss the bull's-eye.

"You can do it, Sadie Rose," Caleb said softly behind her. "God is with you."

"Yes, He is," whispered Sadie. A peace settled over her, and she blocked out the voices around her.

"Ready!" shouted Taylor Jennings.

Sadie lifted her rifle to her shoulder.

"Aim!"

Sadie looked down the long barrel.

"Fire!"

Sadie lined the bull's-eye in her sights and squeezed off a shot, levered another bullet in, squeezed off the second shot, levered again, and shot again. All three shots hit the bull's-eye. Smiling, she lowered her gun. Silently she thanked God for helping her stay calm and shoot straight. She stepped back beside Caleb. "I did it," she said softly.

"That's my Sadie Rose," he said with a wink.

She handed the rifle to Kara and stood quietly as Taylor Jennings called the next row. Kara, Levi Cass, and Red Colvin were three of the contestants. Sadie glanced around until she spotted Sven Johnson. He was talking with a couple of men and didn't even glance at Kara. Sadie frowned. Something strange was indeed going on. But what?

Davis Greavy changed the targets and shouted the numbers of the two who'd hit the bull's-eye all three times. He called her number six, and she swelled with pride. She'd probably make the top ten.

Sadie's ears rang as the next shots were fired. Kara and Red hit the bull's-eye every time. Levi only hit it twice. He walked away, his face red. He wouldn't look at Sadie. She knew he'd find Gerda to make him feel better.

Her eyes sparkling, Kara stepped back to Sadie and handed her the rifle. "I did it," Kara said softly.

"Good work," said Sadie. She watched Red walk away without watching the rest of the match.

The next ones in line included Caleb and Joshua. They both qualified.

"Congratulations, Daddy," said Sadie, smiling up at Caleb.

"It might hurt my pride if you beat me, Sadie Rose."

Sadie chuckled. She knew Caleb was teasing. If she won, he'd be as happy as if he himself had won.

Sadie turned to speak to Kara only to find her gone. Maybe she'd gone to speak to Sven. But Sven and Carl were getting in line for the next shoot, along with Riley and El Hepford. Kara wasn't in sight. With a slight frown Sadie turned back to watch. Sven, Carl, and Riley didn't qualify, but El did.

Taylor Jennings stepped back in front of the shooters who hadn't walked away. He waited for silence, then said, "The names of the ten top shooters are: Sadie York . . ." He smiled stiffly at Sadie. "It seems we got our own Annie Oakley."

Sadie flushed, and everyone laughed.

"Kara Lazlow . . . Another Annie Oakley." Taylor Jennings laughed again. "The other eight are men. Ellis Hepford, Joshua Cass, Caleb York, Red Colvin—of course, Mark Miller, Bill Bird, Tex Parker, and Quint Largo. We'll see all of you here tomorrow to narrow it down to the top five."

Sadie trembled. Did she stand a chance to win the Winchester '76?

Taylor Jennings talked a minute longer, then walked back toward town, with many of the people following him.

Sadie turned to speak to Caleb, but saw him several feet away talking to several men. She hesitated, then walked toward them. She'd walk back to camp with Caleb. Her stomach growled, and she knew it was suppertime.

Just as she reached the circle of men she heard one man say, "Don't that embarrass you to have that girl of yours shooting against you, York?"

Sadie's eyes widened. She'd never thought of that.

Caleb shook his head. "Not a bit. I'm proud of Sadie Rose."

Sadie breathed a sigh of relief.

"It must be hard to support that big family you got stuck with by marryin' that widow woman," said another man.

"It's a fine family," said Caleb.

Sadie took a step back. It hadn't occurred to her that Caleb might feel *stuck* with them. She should leave before they noticed she was there.

"Kids get in the way, though," said a short man with two guns on his hips. "The widow I married has three, and I get thoughts of sendin' them packin'. Don't you never feel that way, York?"

Sadie's heart stood still, and she gripped her rifle tighter.

"I reckon I feel that way from time to time," said Caleb. "A big family is sometimes hard to get used to for an old bachelor like me."

Blood roared in Sadie's ears as she crept away before Caleb knew she'd heard.

How could Caleb feel that way about them? Didn't he love them as much as he'd always said?

Sadie groaned, and tears burned her eyes. Maybe if she won the contest Caleb would be so proud of her he'd never feel stuck with them. And if she won, she'd give the Winchester '76 to Caleb as a gift! Sadie nodded. "Yes! I will win, and I will give the Winchester to Daddy! Then he won't ever feel stuck again!"

7

Secrets

Her head down, Sadie walked away from the light of the campfire and into the shadowy prairie. The supper she'd eaten felt like a ball of lead in her stomach. She hadn't been able to smile when the rest of her family had congratulated her on her shooting. Momma had missed the match because Gerda had insisted they go buy the hat she'd wanted so badly and it had taken longer than expected.

Sadie stopped near the giant cottonwood beside the creek. She heard the trickle of water and smelled the campfires and the different foods that had been cooked. Music filled the air, and several people were dancing.

Sadie leaned against the cottonwood and bit her lower lip. What if she lost the contest? Would

Caleb be so disappointed in her that he'd be even sorrier to have her for a daughter?

A tear slipped down Sadie's cheek, and she quickly brushed it away. She was not a crybaby!

Just then she heard voices and knew someone was coming toward her. She slipped around the tree and stood quietly. She didn't want to see or talk to anyone right now except maybe Mary, her very best friend. But Sadie knew Mary and Jewel were spending the evening with Jewel's friend who lived in Vida.

Sadie suddenly recognized the voices of Sven Johnson and Carl White. Sven was from Sweden and Carl from Switzerland, and they both had heavy accents. Sadie wanted to walk away and not eavesdrop, but if she moved they'd see her and want to talk to her.

"You must speak to her, Sven!" said Carl sternly. "She came all the way from Chicago to marry you."

"She frightens me, Carl," said Sven in an unsteady voice. "She is too pretty! Too little and weak! How can she live like we do?"

Sadie's eyes widened. They were talking about Kara!

"You will build her a house," snapped Carl. "You can't put it off any longer."

"I didn't think she would come."

"But she did come, and you can't let her down."

"She can shoot as well as little Sadie York," said Sven with a chuckle.

"Maybe she is stronger than she looks," said Carl. "She might make a good strong wife for you."

"I am afraid to talk to her."

Sadie bit back a giggle. How could Sven be afraid of Kara? He was usually a very brave man.

"I saw her talk with Red Colvin," said Sven. "Maybe she will want to marry him."

"She might do just that if you don't find her and talk to her," said Carl.

The men walked along the creek, and soon Sadie couldn't hear them. She heard the distant yelp of a coyote and the music from the camp. She glanced up at the sky. Stars seemed to twinkle close enough for her to touch them. The bark of the tree felt rough through her dress, and she started to move just as she heard someone else walking toward her. She bit back a groan and stood very still. She heard a giggle, and her heart sank. It was Gerda! Sadie locked her fingers together. She could not talk to Gerda now!

"You're so sweet, Gabe," said Gerda, giggling again.

Sadie bit back a groan. Gabe and Gerda!

"I don't like you talkin' to Levi Cass so much," said Gabe.

"Are you jealous?" asked Gerda coyly.

"Yes," said Gabe gruffly.

Sadie wanted to step out and tell Gerda to get back to camp, but she stood where she was.

"What will you do if I don't stop seeing Levi?" asked Gerda.

"Walk away from you," said Gabe.

Sadie bit back a laugh. Gerda would never expect Gabe to say that.

"You wouldn't really do that would you, Gabe? I like you a lot, and I don't want you to walk away from me."

"Then stop seeing Levi Cass. He's just a boy anyway."

"Aren't you?"

"I'm eighteen and old enough to marry."

Sadie longed to sneak away, but she couldn't risk it.

"Gerda, girls in Missouri get married at thirteen. Would you?"

"I do like you a lot, Gabe."

"You liked me enough to kiss me."

"I know."

Sadie bit her lip to keep from telling Gabe Gerda was too free and easy with her kisses. If Gabe knew how selfish and lazy Gerda was, he wouldn't want to marry her.

"I will give you another kiss if you want one," said Gerda.

Suddenly without warning Sadie sneezed. She clamped her hand over her nose, but it was too late. Her heart sank to her feet.

"Sadie Rose York!" cried Gerda, rushing over to Sadie and gripping her arm. "How dare you spy on me? Did Levi ask you to?"

"I can't believe you'd do this, Sadie," said Gabe gruffly. "Is Mitch with you? He's good at spying."

Sadie sighed heavily. "I wasn't spying, and Mitch is not with me. I came here to be alone. I heard you and didn't want to talk right now, so I hid. But I didn't think you'd stop right here to talk!"

"I suppose you'll tell your mother about me," said Gerda.

"I'm not a tattletale!"

"If you do tell, I'll tell her about you kissing Mitch," said Gerda sharply.

Sadie doubled her fists at her sides. "Then I'll tell Gabe you're seventeen and not thirteen!" Sadie gasped, and Gerda cried out.

Gabe caught Gerda's arm. "Are you really seventeen?"

"Sadie is lying!" cried Gerda.

"Sadie doesn't lie," said Gabe. "Are you seventeen?"

"She is," said Sadie.

Gerda raised her hand to slap Sadie, but Gabe caught it and held it firmly against his chest.

"So you are seventeen!" Gabe turned to Sadie, but kept Gerda's hand tightly against his chest. "I'll take care of Gerda. You can go now."

"I'll go, but I don't want you to tell anyone else about that terrible kiss!"

"I'll tell everyone!" cried Gerda.

"No, you will not," said Gabe sternly. "Sadie, I'm sorry I told Gerda. I won't tell anyone else. And neither will Gerda."

"I will so!"

"No, you will not! If you do, you know what I'll tell about you."

Gerda bowed her head.

"What about her?" asked Sadie, suddenly very curious.

"Don't you dare tell!" cried Gerda. "It's my secret!"

Gabe laughed softly. "Are you blushing, Gerda?"

Sadie frowned. If the moon were only brighter, she could see if Gerda was really blushing. It wasn't like her. "What is the secret?" asked Sadie.

Gerda jerked her hand away from Gabe and turned to Sadie. "Oh, if you really must know, I'll tell you!" Gerda lifted her chin high. "Mitch has been teaching me how to cook."

Sadie laughed. She'd taught Mitch to cook,

65

and now he was teaching Gerda! "Why don't you want anyone to know?" asked Sadie.

"Ma will make me cook at home," said Gerda. "I'm only learning so I'll know how when I get married."

"So you are thinking about getting married," said Gabe.

"I might be," said Gerda with a toss of her mass of black hair.

"There's a preacher here in Vida," said Gabe. "We could get married while we're here."

Sadie blushed. She didn't want to hear that kind of talk. "I'm goin' back to camp."

"I'll come with you," said Gerda.

"Oh no, you won't!" Gabe caught Gerda and held her to him. "We have some things to settle."

Gerda struggled, laughed softly, then said, "I'll stay a while longer."

Sadie ran away from them before Gerda asked her to wait. Near the first tent she slowed to a walk. She looked around, then frowned. The town kids were huddled at the side of a wagon. The campfire was so bright Sadie could see the kids, but not what they were doing.

Sadie ducked out of sight of the town kids and walked back to her camp. All the Hepfords except Gabe sat around the campfire talking with Sadie's family. She saw the big black feather on Zane Hepford's hat move as he talked. Opal sat beside El, and Sadie wondered if Opal had instigated it or if El had finally found the courage. Redheaded Vard sat between Helen and Web. Vard's pa, Judge Loggia, sat on one side of Caleb and Zane Hepford on the other side. Kara Lazlow sat beside Momma. Kara glanced up as Sadie stepped into view. They smiled at each other as Sadie sat in an empty spot beside Mitch.

"I wondered where you were," said Mitch in a low voice that only Sadie could hear.

"Off by myself," said Sadie. She couldn't look at Caleb in case he was looking at her and could read her thoughts.

"I watched you shoot," said Mitch quietly to keep from disturbing his pa while he talked about his pa fighting in the War Between the States. "You did real good."

"Thank you," said Sadie, thankful for his praise.

"Did you see Red Colvin?"

Sadie nodded.

"I don't know if you can beat him."

Sadie sighed. "I don't know either, but I'll try."

"I heard him and Quint Largo fighting outside the livery a while ago. They sure hate each other."

Sadie glanced at Kara and saw that she'd heard what Mitch had said.

In a low tight voice Kara said, "Excuse me please." She jumped up and disappeared into the darkness.

"I have to talk to Kara, Mitch. See you later." Sadie slipped away from the circle and ran after Kara.

Suddenly Sadie tripped over something and sprawled to the ground. She heard giggling, and she pushed herself up. The town kids stood over her, laughing at her.

Miles shouted, "I tripped the thief! Hey, everybody! I caught the girl stealing the money!" He ducked down and stuffed a wad of bills into her hand.

Sadie tried to jump up, but Jake pushed her back to the ground. Fear stung her skin.

Just then several men with lanterns ran into sight.

"We caught the thief!" cried Miles, pointing down at Sadie.

"Over here, Papa! She took the money!" said Amy, waving her arms.

One of the men stepped forward. Sadie saw it was Taylor Jennings, the mayor, and her heart turned over. What if he believed the town kids?

"What's going on here?" asked Caleb as he strode up.

Sadie jumped up and huddled against Caleb. "They said I took some money, but I didn't!"

"She did!" cried the town kids.

"It's there!" said Miles excitedly as he pointed to the ground.

"She dropped it right where she fell!" snapped Taylor Jennings as he reached down for the wad of bills. "This is serious business, young lady." He looked closer at her. "Why, you're the little Annie Oakley!"

"I did not steal the money," Sadie said weakly.

"She wouldn't steal," said Caleb in a firm voice.

"Is this your daughter?" asked the mayor.

"Yes."

"Not his real daughter, Papa," said Amy as she tucked her hand in the mayor's hand. "His step-daughter."

Sadie frowned, and she felt Caleb stiffen. "I didn't do it, Daddy," whispered Sadie through a dry throat. "They put the money in my hand."

"Now why would they do that?" asked Taylor Jennings impatiently. "These are good kids here. Two of 'em are mine."

Shivers ran up and down Sadie's spine as she clung to Caleb's work-roughened hand.

"I want this settled," said Caleb in a commanding voice. "I don't want any black mark against Sadie Rose's name."

"We got the money back, so we won't press charges," said the mayor. "But you folks will have to leave town first thing in the morning."

"No!" cried Sadie, shaking her head. She couldn't leave before she'd had a try at winning the Winchester '76 for Caleb.

"First thing in the morning," said Taylor Jennings sternly. "If you're still here by noon, I'll fine you fifty dollars."

Sadie gasped. They didn't have fifty dollars. What could she do to make the town kids tell the truth? She looked at their smug faces, and her heart sank.

8

The Decision

Sadie slowly walked back to camp with Caleb. "I didn't steal any money, Daddy," she said with a catch in her voice.

"I know," said Caleb with a heavy sigh.

"What happened?" asked Momma as she ducked out of the tent. The Hepfords were gone, and the family was settling for the night. They all joined Momma when they heard the concern in her voice.

"Somebody stole money from the Vida Days cash box," said Caleb. "They blamed Sadie."

"What?" cried Momma, bristling. "Why would they say such a terrible thing?"

Sadie quickly told them the whole story and finished by explaining, "The town kids have been mad at me since this afternoon, so they were trying to get back at me."

"The mayor wouldn't listen," said Caleb. "It's their word against ours."

Momma helplessly shook her head.

"We have to leave in the morning," said Caleb.

"Leave?" the kids cried, looking at Sadie as if it were all her fault.

"Let's get to bed and talk about it in the morning," said Momma. "This has been a long day."

Sadie knew the others wanted to talk but wouldn't because Momma had spoken.

The next morning Sadie looked at her family as they stood around the campfire talking about what to do. They were all looking at her. Was Caleb wishing he'd never married Momma with her big family? Tears burned the backs of Sadie's eyes, but she wouldn't let them fall.

"I won't go home!" cried Gerda, stamping her foot. "I don't care what you say! I will not go home!"

"Gerda, this is not the time to think of yourself," said Caleb with a stern look.

Gerda clamped her mouth closed and stepped back away from the others. "I'll go talk to Gabe. He'll help me!" She flipped back her long hair and walked away. Nobody tried to stop her.

Sadie moved from one foot to the other. She knew Helen and Web were bursting with things to say. She also knew they wouldn't say anything until they were alone with her. Last night both Helen and Opal had tried to question Sadie, but Momma had stopped them with a stern word.

"I want to speak to Taylor Jennings," said Momma, squaring her sturdy shoulders and looking very determined. "He can't accuse Sadie of stealing and get by with it."

"He won't believe us," said Caleb as he slipped

an arm around Momma. "His own kids lied to him. He won't admit to that."

"I'll find those kids and make them tell the truth," said Momma grimly.

"It's not worth it," said Caleb, sounding very tired.

Sadie forced back a sob. Wasn't she worth fighting for?

"We'll go home where we belong." Caleb started to turn away, but Momma caught his arm and pulled him back.

"We won't leave in defeat!" Momma's dark eyes flashed with fire.

Sadie stared in shock at Momma. She had always done exactly what Caleb said.

"What can we do?" asked Caleb softly. "I don't know what to do when it comes to kids."

Sadie sucked in her breath. Was it possible that Caleb didn't know everything?

Momma looked around at her family. "We're going to prove Sadie didn't steal that money. I want all of you to walk around town and keep your eyes and ears open. If you hear or see anything that'll help Sadie, come back here and tell me."

"Yes, Momma," they all said.

Sadie couldn't get a sound through her tight throat.

Just then Kara walked up. Sadie hadn't realized she was gone. She'd slept in the tent last night. She must've gotten up earlier than any of them to slip out without being seen.

"I talked to Red Colvin about what happened to Sadie," said Kara. "He said he'd help clear her name."

Sadie's eyes widened in surprise.

"Do you know Red Colvin?" asked Caleb.

Kara hesitated, then nodded. "I knew he was going to be at Vida Days. That's why I came."

Sadie felt weak all over. Just what was going on between Red and Kara?

Momma cleared her throat. "I thought you came to marry Sven Johnson."

Kara flushed. "I did. But I also came to see Red." Kara fingered the cameo at her throat. "I'd rather not talk about me. I want to help you. You've all been so kind to me."

Sadie looked off across the camp at all the tents and wagons. Could she face everyone, knowing they thought she'd stolen money from Vida Days proceeds? She glanced back at Momma's set face, and she knew she didn't have a choice. Momma had made up her mind. Caleb still looked uncertain, but he would listen to Momma. Before Pa died in the blizzard, whatever he said was law. Nobody could say or do different. But Caleb wasn't like that. Right now Sadie wished he was. She didn't want to see the looks or hear the whispers. She wanted to go back to the Circle Y Ranch where she was safe.

Momma retied her bonnet. Suddenly she looked ten feet tall instead of short and plump. "I want all of you to eat breakfast, then walk around and see what you can see and hear. We'll meet back here no later than mid-morning even if we haven't discovered anything. We have only until noon, so we must hurry. Sadie, it would be best if you stay here. And remember this—God is with us!"

Momma sounded so confident that Sadie felt a little better. She ate the cornmeal mush Opal had fixed, then helped Helen wash the bowls and put them away in a box in the wagon.

Helen sighed loud and long. "Sadie, I wish I

could have adventures like you do. I never get to do anything exciting."

Sadie hugged Helen. "I hope you never have somebody say you stole something."

Helen's face fell. "I hate being the youngest! Everyone always takes care of me so nothing can happen to me."

Caleb settled his hat in place as he walked up to Sadie. "I'll find Joshua Cass and tell him what happened. He represents the law in these parts, so maybe he can help."

"I hope he can," said Sadie.

"Keep your chin up, Sadie Rose," Caleb said in his soft Texas drawl.

Sadie smiled slightly and nodded. She wanted Caleb to pull her close and tell her he loved her, but he walked away.

Several minutes later, after the family had left, Sadie watched Mitch running toward her where she sat on the ground beside the wagon. He was wearing his new boots as well as the same overalls and shirt he'd worn yesterday. He hadn't brushed his hair. She jumped up and waited, the strings of her bonnet dangling from her hand.

"I just heard what happened to you!" he said as he slid to a stop beside her. "I came to help."

"Thanks, Mitch."

"I heard Gerda tell Gabe what had happened. At first I didn't believe her. I thought maybe she just wanted to get rid of me so she could be alone with Gabe." Mitch grinned and shrugged. "I know she's your cousin, but she does lie sometimes."

"I know. It's a great embarrassment to us all."

Mitch leaned back against the wagon and wrapped his fingers around his suspenders. "Tell me about these town kids. Why did they pick on you?"

Sadie looked off across the camp at the children running around, the men and women working and talking, and a fiddler playing a merry tune. Smoke from campfires drifted up to the bright blue sky. Finally Sadie turned back to Mitch and told him about the first time she'd seen the town kids and about pushing Jake down.

Mitch doubled his fists, and a muscle jumped in his jaw. "I'll find Jake and knock him clear into next week!"

"He's bigger than you, Mitch."

"I don't care! I'll get El to help me."

Just then Sadie saw the town kids sneaking around a nearby wagon. She counted seven of them, three girls and four boys. Her heart stopped, then hammered loud enough for Mitch to hear. She gripped his arm. "Here they come," she whispered hoarsely.

Mitch spotted them. "I can't take 'em all on at once," he said in a low, tight voice. Suddenly he dashed away, leaving Sadie to face the town kids alone. She wanted to yell for him to come back, but she didn't want to make a sound and give her location away to the town kids.

Sadie glanced toward the tent. Should she hide inside? She scowled at the cowardly thought. She'd face them. She darted a look around, but suddenly noticed the other campers had left, probably to get good seats at the rodeo that would be starting soon.

Just then the town kids spied Sadie, and her mouth turned bone-dry. What were they going to do to her? She watched as they huddled in a circle. She knew they were making plans. Oh, what should she do? She could outrun them easily. But what good would that do? She'd have to face them sooner or later.

Slowly Sadie stepped away from the wagon and boldly faced the town kids. Her knees knocked, and shivers ran up and down her spine. She locked her knees and stood with her head high and her hands at her sides. A bee buzzed around her, but she ignored it. In the distance people cheered as the rodeo got under way. "What do you want with me?" she asked before they reached her.

"My pa said you were to get out of town," said Miles. "Why are you still here?"

"Because I'm not leaving," said Sadie, forcing her voice to stay steady. "I didn't take the money, and you all know it."

"Nobody will believe you," said Jake as he stepped forward, grinning. "We made sure of that."

"Why are you doing this to me?" cried Sadie.

Amy stepped forward, the white bows on her braids swaying against her shoulders. "You country kids think you're better than we are! You're not! We're smarter and look better. We don't have to be little Annie Oakleys to prove we're better!"

Just then Sadie saw Red Colvin ride up several feet behind the town kids. Sadie's pulse leaped, but she didn't let it show. Red slipped from his Appaloosa and walked silently toward the kids.

"I never said I was better," said Sadie. She raised her voice. "And you know I didn't steal the money." She jabbed her finger at Miles. "You stuffed it in my hand! You know you did."

"So what?" Miles shrugged. "Nobody will believe it."

"I will," said Red Colvin.

The town kids spun around, gasping in surprise.

"I heard you admit you framed Sadie," said Red. "You know the town people will believe me when I tell them the truth."

Sadie smiled in relief.

The town kids groaned.

Red waved his hand. "You run along and tell your pa you were playing a joke on Sadie York. Make him take back what he said about the York family leavin' town. I want to be able to shoot against this little mite."

Just then Mitch and Zane Hepford strode around the tent, Taylor Jennings between them. Jennings looked mad enough to spit nails. Sadie could tell Mitch was pleased with himself, and Zane was ready for a fight. The Missouri family liked a good fight.

Zane stopped Jennings beside Sadie. "Look at them kids pickin' on little Sadie York," said Zane. "You call that an even fight, mayor?"

Jennings flushed as he looked from the kids to Red Colvin. "What's the meaning of this?"

"Your kids have something to tell you," said Red. He narrowed his eyes as he looked at Amy and Miles. "Tell your pa the truth."

Sadie smiled at Mitch, then watched the town kids squirm as Miles told Jennings what they'd done.

"We were just playin' a joke on her," said Amy. "Honest, Pa."

"Just a joke," said Miles weakly.

"You carried it too far," said Jennings gruffly. "You embarrassed me. I want you to get home and stay there." He turned back to Sadie. "You find your family and tell them they can stay."

78

Sadie nodded.

"Not so fast, mayor," said Red. "*You* find the family and tell them. You smeared their good name. It's only right you set the record straight."

A muscle jumped in Jennings's jaw, but he nodded. "I'll tell them."

"Next time you think you can make trouble, you think of me," said Zane Hepford, his black feather bobbing in his hat as he talked. "I take it real personal when you hurt a friend of mine."

Jennings swallowed hard. "I am sorry."

Sadie stood quietly while Jennings and the town kids walked away. Zane tipped his hat to Sadie, then strode after Jennings.

"They shouldn't cause any more trouble for you," said Red.

Sadie smiled up at the big man. "Thanks for helpin' me."

"Any time." Red winked at Sadie. "See you at the shootin' range."

Sadie nodded, her heart bursting with thanksgiving as Red strode to his Appaloosa and rode away. Finally she turned to Mitch. He was watching Red with narrowed eyes.

"You watch out for Red Colvin," said Mitch. "He's trouble."

Sadie stiffened. "He's my friend," she said. But was there something about Red that she needed to know? What if he was trouble for her too?

9
Gerda

After dinner Sadie settled her wide-brimmed black hat in place and was ready to go with Helen and Web to watch the roping contest.

"Sadie Rose, come here," called Caleb from where he stood at the front of the wagon.

Sadie hesitated. Caleb didn't have his usual smile on his face. He hadn't seemed as pleased as she thought he'd be when he'd learned everything was settled with the stolen money and that they were free to stay. Maybe he'd want to leave anyway. She plucked nervously at her calico skirt as she slowly walked to him.

"Gerda didn't show up for dinner," said Caleb with a scowl. "She doesn't know we're staying. Go find her and let her know."

Sadie wanted to refuse, but she nodded. She looked longingly after Web and Helen, then headed toward the Hepfords' wagon. She spotted Levi Cass leading his black mare Netty toward the creek. "Levi!" she called.

He turned with a flush, then smiled when he saw it was Sadie. He was tall and lean and was dressed like a cowboy. He pushed his hat to the back of his head and waited for Sadie. "Howdy," he said as if he was glad to see her.

"Are you headin' for the horse race?" asked Sadie.

Levi nodded. "You comin' to watch?" He already knew she wouldn't be in it because she'd had to leave Apple at home.

"I have to find Gerda first. Have you seen her?"

Levi's face hardened. "No! And I don't want to."

"Why? What happened?" asked Sadie, angry that Gerda had hurt Levi.

"She's been flirtin' with every cowboy she set her eyes on. I told her I wouldn't have it, but she just laughed and walked away." Levi sighed. "I don't know why I thought I loved her."

Sadie's heart leaped. "She saved your life."

"If she thinks she can flirt with any man she sets her eyes on, then I don't want her even hangin' around me. I'm done with her."

Sadie bit back a smile. "You are?"

"I'm done with all women!" Levi tipped his hat and led Netty away.

Sadie watched him go. "Now we can be friends again," she muttered, then smiled.

A few minutes later Sadie stopped at the Hepfords' wagon. The boys were cleaning up after dinner, and Zane lay under the wagon, his hat over his face.

"Is Gerda here?" asked Sadie.

"No," said Mitch.

"She didn't show up for dinner," said Sadie. "Caleb sent me to find her."

"She's not been here since just after breakfast," said Gabe, looking worried. "I'll help you find her."

Zane pulled his hat off his face and said, "You can't go, Gabe. We have to practice."

Gabe frowned. "We're playin' for everybody tonight after supper."

"I don't mind goin' alone," said Sadie.

"Maybe she's with Levi Cass," said Gabe, his shoulders drooping.

"She's not," said Sadie. "I already talked to him."

Gabe brightened. "She was put out with me some this mornin'."

"I'm sure I'll find her soon."

"If you don't, come get me," said Gabe.

"I will." Sadie said good-bye and ran down by the creek. She had to find Gerda before it was time to go to the shooting range for the sharpshooter contest. "Gerda won't make me miss that!" said Sadie grimly. She had to make the top five!

Sadie saw several kids playing at the creek, and she asked them if they'd seen Gerda. They hadn't, so she headed into town, asking each person she saw. No one had seen her, and if they had, it had been just after breakfast.

Dust billowed out behind a wagon pulled by two draft horses and settled on Sadie. She slapped it off with her hat. The noise all around her made her wish she was back at the Circle Y. If it wasn't for the shooting contest, she'd be ready to leave now.

Sadie walked up and down the crowded sidewalks and into each store, but she couldn't find

Gerda. "Where is she?" muttered Sadie as she stood at the edge of town and looked toward the crowd gathered to watch the horse race. She saw Riley on Bay with Levi beside him on Netty. Carl White was astride his great white stallion, Marengo, and Sven was beside him on his roan, Traveler. About ten others had entered the race. Riley looked excited . . . and determined to win. Sadie hoped he would, but she also wanted Levi to win.

Slowly Sadie walked around the crowd. She saw Kara glance at Sven, then look quickly away. Sadie knew the two still hadn't spoken to each other. Opal had said she was going to step in and get them together before nightfall if they didn't manage on their own.

Taylor Jennings fired the starter gun and the horses leaped ahead, leaving a cloud of dust and a thundering of hooves. Shouts from the crowd were so loud they could probably be heard all the way to Dakota Territory.

Sadie wanted to stay to see who won, but with a sigh she walked back into town. The streets were almost empty.

"Sadie!"

Sadie turned, then laughed happily to see Mary Ferguson running toward her. Mary's copper-brown braids hung down from her calico sunbonnet and bounced on her slender shoulders. Dust puffed up on her brown shoes. She wore a calico dress Sadie hadn't seen before. "I'm glad to see you, Mary!"

"And you! Where're you going?" asked Mary in her English accent.

Sadie wrinkled her nose. "To find Gerda."

"I'll go with you."

"Thank you."

As they walked, Sadie told Mary all that had happened. She even told her about Caleb. "Mary, I don't think he really wants us kids." Sadie's voice broke, and she swallowed hard.

Mary shook her head. "That can't be! He is full of love!"

Sadie felt a little better, but she knew what she'd heard, and she'd seen the look on Caleb's face.

After the second time up and down the main street with Mary, Sadie stopped and frowned. "I get so tired looking out for Gerda!"

"She *is* family, Sadie," said Mary softly, her brown eyes glistening with tears. All of Mary's family had died in an epidemic. Disguised as an orphan boy, she'd lived a hard life, until Jewel had taken her in. "Family is important, Sadie."

"I know. And Gerda is Momma's Michigan cousin." Sadie glanced around and then up at the two-story wood-frame boardinghouse. Gerda stood at one of the closed windows, a frightened look on her face! She was frantically waving to Sadie.

"There she is!" cried Sadie, pointing up.

Mary turned to look. "What is she doing?"

"We better go see," said Sadie impatiently, but she didn't move.

Suddenly Gerda covered her mouth and jumped back. The curtain dropped in place.

"She's strange," said Mary.

The hairs on the back of Sadie's neck stood on end. She knew somebody was watching her. Slowly she turned. A fat man stood just outside the hardware store, and he was looking right at her. He wore a black suit and white shirt. The short jacket of his suit fit tight across his shoulders and wouldn't button over his stomach. He narrowed his eyes, then slowly turned away. Sadie gasped. It was the very man who had tried to get Gerda to kiss him behind the feed store!

"Do you know that man, Mary?" whispered Sadie.

"His name is Nash Hubert, but I don't know him. I met him last night at the Beekers' place with Jewel. He stopped in to talk to Pad Beeker about hiring a buggy for today."

"He scares me," said Sadie as they hurried toward the boardinghouse. A bell over the door tinkled as they walked inside. Narrow stairs that led to the second floor stood beside the front desk. A man not much older than Riley stood behind the desk, leaning on the counter. He was reading a dime novel with a picture of an Indian scalping a man.

Sadie and Mary started up the stairs.

"Hold it!" snapped the man, dropping his book on the counter. "You can't just walk up there without an okay from me. I'm Rob, and I'm in charge today."

"We came to see Gerda Tasker," said Sadie, gripping the shiny banister and looking down at the man.

Rob shook his head. "She's not registered here."

"But I saw her standing at a window," said Sadie. "She's my cousin, and I want to talk to her."

"We won't stay long," said Mary.

Rob hesitated, then shrugged and picked up his book. "Go on up."

Sadie ran up the stairs with Mary at her heels. Suddenly Sadie stopped. "I don't know what room she's in."

Mary frowned thoughtfully. "I think it would be

down there." She pointed down the narrow hall. Sunlight shone through an open window at the end of the gray hallway. Hot wind blew in and stirred the stale air that smelled of cigar smoke.

Sadie's heels clicked loudly on the wooden floor as she walked down the hall. She knocked on a door, but no one answered. She flushed painfully. Would she have to knock on every door until she found Gerda?

Mary stopped. "Gerda!" she called.

Sadie caught Mary's arm and said, "Shhh! What will folks think?"

"Sadie! Mary!"

Sadie heard Gerda's muffled voice behind the door to her left. She ran to it. "Gerda, open the door."

"I can't! I'm locked in!"

Sadie gasped.

"Where's the key?" asked Mary as she rattled the brass doorknob.

Gerda didn't answer.

"Where's the key, Gerda?" asked Sadie impatiently.

"That man took it!" cried Gerda, bursting into tears. "He locked me in, and he's coming back for me. I saw him behind you on the street!"

"Nash Hubert?" asked Mary.

"Yes!" Gerda sobbed harder. "Get me out! Hurry before he returns! He's going to take me with him, and I don't want to go!"

Sadie shivered. How could she get the key? If Nash Hubert caught them helping Gerda, what would he do? Sadie ran to the window and looked out onto the street. Nash Hubert was walking toward the boardinghouse! Her heart plunged to her feet. "He's coming, Mary! What shall we do?"

"We'll have to get the key from the guy at the desk." Mary ran down the hall toward the stairs, her feet loud in the hallway.

"We'll be right back, Gerda," said Sadie against the door.

"Don't leave me!" cried Gerda.

Sadie hesitated, then ran after Mary.

Mary stopped at the desk, her cheeks red and her dark eyes flashing. "We found Gerda Tasker, but she's locked in! We need a key to get her out!"

Rob frowned. "You must be mistaken."

"We just talked to her," said Sadie.

Mary leaned against the tall counter. "Do you want us to call for help? Do you want us to scream and scream and have people run in here to see what's wrong?"

Rob sighed and pulled the key from a drawer. "I'll unlock the door myself. But this better not be a trick."

Sadie watched the front door, her pulse racing. "We have to hurry!" She dashed after Mary up the stairs. Rob seemed to take forever just to reach the landing. Sadie heard the bell downstairs tinkle over the outside door. Fear pricked her skin, and she couldn't breathe.

"Which room?" asked Rob, hiking up his pants.

"This one!" cried Sadie as she ran to the door. "Gerda, we're back!"

"Get me out of here!" Gerda cried, thumping the door.

"I'll be jiggered," said Rob as he slowly stuck the key in the lock and turned it.

With a sob Gerda opened the door and jumped out, grabbing Sadie as if she'd never let go.

"He's coming," said Mary. "We have to leave now." She turned to Rob. "Is there another way out?"

"Nope."

Just then Nash Hubert reached the top of the stairs. He glared down the hallway at the girls and Rob. "How dare you unlock my door!"

"This girl got locked in," said Rob nervously.

"She was there of her own accord," snapped Nash Hubert.

"No, I wasn't!" cried Gerda.

Sadie trembled. Silently she prayed for help. She remembered Kara and her hat pin, but Sadie knew none of them had a hat pin. "My pa is Caleb York, and he sent me to get Gerda," said Sadie. "If I don't bring her back, he'll come lookin' for us."

Hubert's face paled. "You tell him she came up here of her own free will." Hubert shook his fat finger at Gerda. "You tell him that or you'll be sorry!"

Her eyes wide, Gerda cringed against Sadie. "He said he had a yellow parasol he'd give me . . . one that would match my yellow dress."

Sadie shook her head in disgust.

"We're leaving," said Mary firmly. She led the way, and Sadie and Gerda followed.

Sadie admired the calm way Mary walked past Hubert. Her legs trembling, Sadie led Gerda past the man. Sadie smelled his sweat and felt his anger. It seemed to take an hour just to reach the stairs.

Out on the street Sadie breathed a sigh of relief.

Gerda stopped short. "I want to go home! I want to go home right now!"

Sadie's heart sank. Would Momma say they had to leave just because Gerda wanted to?

10
The Top Five

Sadie stood beside the tent while Gerda talked to Momma and Caleb inside. They'd just returned from watching the horse race. Carl White had won.

Mary squeezed Sadie's hand and whispered, "I have to go. Jewel said to find her right after the race. Let me know if you have to go home."

Sadie nodded. She couldn't speak around the lump in her throat. It wouldn't be fair if they had to leave just because Gerda wanted to.

Sadie kicked at a clump of grass, then leaned back against the wagon. From the rope corral near the creek she heard a horse whinny. A hawk soared high in the huge blue sky.

Finally Caleb ducked out of the tent. His face was dark with anger. He strode away without a word to Sadie. She bit her lip and rubbed her sweaty palms down her patched dress.

Momma ducked out of the tent, smoothing her hair back. Her cheeks were red, and her eyes flashing with anger. She saw Sadie, and she tried to control her emotions. "Isn't it time for the shooting match, Sadie?" asked Momma stiffly.

Sadie nodded. "Do we have to go home now?" she asked just above a whisper.

"No," said Momma crisply. "Go to the shooting match. I'll stay with Gerda."

Her heart thudding, Sadie grabbed the rifle from the wagon and ran toward the shooting range. She desperately wanted to know what had happened in the tent, but she knew she couldn't ask. And even if she did ask, Momma wouldn't tell her.

Sadie heard the pounding of hooves, and she glanced up to see a horse and rider bearing down on her. She jumped aside, and the horse thundered past. The rider was Quint Largo, the big bearded man Red Colvin didn't like. But where was Quint Largo going? It was time to shoot, and he was in the top ten.

Sadie walked up to the crowd already gathered to watch the shoot. She saw some of the shooters. Where was Caleb? Even Kara wasn't there, nor Red Colvin. What was going on?

Sadie stopped beside Joshua Cass. He was tall and wide with dark hair and eyes. He smiled at Sadie, and she smiled back.

"Where's York?" asked Joshua.

Sadie shrugged. Joshua couldn't get used to calling him Caleb. He'd only had a last name until recently when he decided he wanted two names like everyone else. The Texas rancher who'd found him as a baby crying under a cactus had named him York after the place in England where he'd come from. Momma and Opal had given him his first name after Caleb in the Bible. "I thought he'd be here by now."

"I reckon you found Gerda?"

Sadie nodded.

"Good." Joshua rubbed his jaw and narrowed his eyes. "That one is a troublemaker." He grinned. "I don't mean to bad-mouth her. I know she's your cousin, and I respect that."

"She's with Momma at camp."

"Good place for her."

Just then Caleb walked up. He smiled and tugged Sadie's braid. "Shoot the middle right out of that bull's-eye today, Sadie Rose."

Sadie's heart lightened, and she smiled. "I will, Daddy! You too."

"What about me?" asked Joshua with a wink.

Sadie giggled. "You too."

"But we can't all win," said Caleb. "Look how far away the targets are today. And tomorrow they'll be even farther back."

Sadie looked at the targets, but she knew she could easily hit the bull's-eye three times unless something dreadful happened to her.

Just then Red Colvin strode up, his face a thundercloud.

Sadie trembled. She'd heard he had a temper, but she'd never seen it before. What had happened to upset him so much? Would he be too upset to shoot straight? Her heart leaped at the thought of not having to compete with Red, but then she frowned. She did not want Red out of the contest unless he was out fair and square.

Taylor Jennings called for attention, and gradually everyone grew quiet.

Sadie listened to his speech while she glanced around for Kara. Only Kara and Quint Largo were missing. What would happen if they didn't make it in time? Would the mayor wait for them?

Sadie turned back and listened as Jennings explained about the change in the distance. He made it sound too far away to hit. The crowd clapped and cheered his speech.

"Sadie," whispered Kara.

Sadie turned in relief. Kara looked as if she'd been crying. "Is something wrong, Kara?" asked Sadie softly.

Kara shrugged. "Nothing I can talk about, but I'll be all right. Can I use your gun again?"

Sadie nodded. She started to speak again, but a shot rang out, and the words died in her throat.

Quint Largo reined in his horse, his smoking six-gun pointed to the sky. "I reckon I'm right on time," he yelled. He dropped to the ground, holstered his gun, and pulled his rifle from the boot of his saddle.

Sadie glanced at Red and saw his jaw tighten.

"Time to begin!" called Taylor Jennings. "The first five shooters are Sadie York, Red Colvin, Joshua Cass, El Hepford, and Bill Bird."

"God is with you, Sadie Rose," whispered Caleb, smiling reassuringly at Sadie.

"I know," said Sadie. She took a deep breath and stepped to the line. El stood on one side of her and Bill Bird on the other.

"Shoot straight, Little Annie Oakley!" people from the crowd called.

Sadie trembled, then took a deep breath. She couldn't let anything distract her. The sun felt hot on her head, but she ignored it.

Sadie listened for the call to fire. She lifted the rifle to her shoulder, aimed, and fired her three shots. She was sure each one hit the bull's-eye, but she wouldn't know for sure until Davis Greavy called her number.

"Good luck, Sadie," said El softly, his face red. He was almost too shy to look at her, but he smiled and she smiled back.

"You too," she said. Her nerves tense, she waited for Davis Greavy to announce the results.

Greavy called out the numbers on the targets that had three shots through the bull's-eye. Her number was called, and she laughed in delight. She listened as El and Red were named too.

"You did it again, Sadie Rose," said Caleb proudly.

Sadie felt as if she were going to burst as she nodded. Silently she thanked God for helping her. Maybe she would win tomorrow. She could see herself getting the Winchester, then giving it to Caleb with a long speech about what a good pa he was to all of them.

"I need your rifle, Sadie," said Kara, holding out her hand.

Sadie jerked herself back to reality and handed the rifle to Kara.

Kara took the rifle and aimed it at Quint Largo's back. Sadie froze. She thought Kara was going to shoot Largo on the spot. Finally Kara lowered the rifle, took her place on the line, and waited to shoot.

Sadie watched Kara, Caleb, Mark Miller, Quint Largo, and Tex Parker shoot. The sound almost deafened her. The smell of gunpowder stung her nose.

Finally Caleb stepped back beside her. "I think I missed," he said with a sigh.

"Wait and see," she said. She didn't know what she'd do if she won and he lost.

Looking grim, Kara handed the rifle to Sadie. "I was too tense," she said.

Sadie tried to comfort Kara, but nothing she said helped.

At last Davis Greavy called out, "Only one person shot three shots in the bull's-eye . . . number eleven!"

"That's me!" whispered Kara, her hand over her heart.

Taylor Jennings shouted, "Kara Lazlow." When the clapping died down he said, "Bring the targets so we can choose the fifth person."

Suddenly Quint dropped his rifle with a roar and flung himself at Red Colvin. "You bent my sights!"

Red's rifle flew from his hand, and he fell on his back with a grunt, with Largo on top of him. They tussled on the ground, tearing tough prairie grass up by the roots and sending sand spraying.

Startled, Sadie jumped back out of the way.

Joshua Cass and Caleb leaped on the men and pulled Largo off Red. "No fightin', boys!" snapped Joshua. "Settle this later away from here."

Red jumped up and would've leaped on Largo, but Caleb held him back. Both men swore, and Joshua commanded them to stop.

Kara stepped close to Red and whispered something to him that Sadie couldn't hear. Red calmed down, and finally Caleb set him free.

"Now let's get on with the show!" shouted Taylor Jennings, his face red. Everyone grew quiet. "I have looked over the targets, and I find that Greavy made a mistake. We have our fifth shooter for tomorrow." Jennings looked around and waited until the tension was almost at a breaking point. "The fifth shooter is Quint Largo! His shots were so close together that Davis thought he'd hit only twice." A cheer rose, then quieted almost immediately. "Tomorrow at 5 we'll have the final shoot to see who takes home the Winchester '76. The top five winners are: Sadie York, Kara Lazlow, El Hepford, Quint Largo, and of course, Red Colvin!"

Sadie swelled with pride while several people patted her on the back and shoulder.

"We've had some fine shootin' here," said Jennings. "Top notch! You should all be real proud of yourselves. See you here tomorrow for the final shoot! If one of you in the finals don't show up, you're out without question."

"That's pretty harsh, mayor," a man from the crowd called.

Jennings spread his hands wide. "Them's the rules, folks. See you all tomorrow!"

As the crowd cheered Sadie saw Sven Johnson walking hesitantly toward Kara.

"Oh no!" whispered Kara. "Not yet!" She turned and ran away, her skirts flapping about her ankles.

Sadie saw the stunned look on Sven's face as he stopped, then turned away. She wanted to run to him to say something to make him feel better, but she didn't have any idea what to say. Maybe Caleb could help Sven.

Sadie turned to speak to Caleb, but he was gone too. Her heart sank. Was he feeling bad because she'd beaten him?

Sadie groaned, and her eyes filled with hot tears. A tear slipped down her cheek and landed in the dust at her feet.

11

Around the Campfire

Yawning, Sadie sat in the shadow of their wagon. A crowd of people gathered around the high campfire Riley had built just after dark. Stars twinkled in the sky. People laughed and talked as they found places on the ground to spread quilts and sit. Up high in the back of their wagon the Hepfords tuned their instruments. The squack of Mitch's fiddle made the most noise. The black cloud over Sadie seemed to grow even darker. Caleb hadn't spoken to her all evening. But then he'd been gone except while they ate venison stew and biscuits.

Just then Mary sat down beside Sadie. "I looked all over for you, Sadie. What's wrong? I know you did well in the shooting contest. Is it Gerda again?"

"No . . . Yes . . . It's more than Gerda. She's been quiet since we brought her back."

"Maybe she finally learned her lesson."

"Maybe." Sadie hoped so, but she knew how stubborn Gerda could be.

Suddenly Mary grabbed Sadie's arm. "Look!" Mary whispered. "Sven is trying to get up the courage to speak to Kara."

Sadie watched Sven walk up beside Kara with his hat in his hands. She heard him say, "Howdy. I am Sven Johnson."

Kara jumped up from her quilt and said, "Bess needs my help." She dashed away before Sven could say another word.

Sven clamped his hat on and walked into the darkness.

"I don't understand Kara at all," said Mary. "She came to marry Sven, but she won't even talk to him."

"I wish somebody would tell us what's goin' on," said Sadie with a long sigh. "But we're kids, and nobody will tell us."

Just then the Hepfords struck up a lively tune that set Sadie's toes tapping. They stood in the back of the wagon playing their instruments. Zane played banjo, El guitar, Gabe a hammered dulcimer, Mitch a fiddle, and five-year-old Vard a mouth organ. The music drifted out across the camp and over the tents and the rope corral out into the prairie on one side and into the town on the other side.

Vard's pa, Judge Loggia, jumped up in the back of the wagon just as they started playing "We're Marching to Zion." Judge lifted his voice and sang the words, sending a tingle of delight over Sadie. Nobody could sing like Judge Loggia!

Sadie pulled her knees to her chin and wrapped her arms around her legs as she listened to Judge sing song after song. Finally he asked everyone to join in, and Sadie jumped up and sang from the bottom of her heart while Mary stood beside her and sang just as enthusiastically.

At the end of the singing, Judge bowed while everyone clapped, then sat back down. "We got us a real honest-to-goodness preacher man here tonight," Judge said. "Our family has been meetin' together for singin', Bible readin' and prayin' at the Circle Y, so it's a real pleasure to hear a preacher." Judge laughed as he looked down at Caleb. "Nothin' personal, Caleb." Everyone laughed, and then Judge motioned to a man standing up. "Brother Zach, come up here and say a few words."

Sadie watched the preacher climb up on the wagon. He wore a black suit and carried a big Bible. He looked small standing next to Judge Loggia and was no older than Sven Johnson and Carl White. He was a traveling preacher and had came in special for Vida Days to marry the folks who were planning on tying the knot.

"I'm glad to be here with all of you tonight," said Brother Zach in a pleasant deep voice. "After that glorious singin' I feel right close to Heaven." He opened his Bible. "I want to read about the three Hebrew men thrown in the fiery furnace when they wouldn't bow to an idol." He closed the Bible, with his finger marking his place, and held it high over his head. With his chin up he shouted, "We don't bow to idols! We serve God Almighty and bow only to Him!"

Sadie's heart swelled as she listened to the preacher. Twice she almost shouted "Amen" like some of the others were doing. She knew more than anything else she wanted to live for God only and worship only Him. She knew He was watching over her always and would protect her just as He had the young men who came out of the furnace without even smelling of smoke. God was a great God! He was her Heavenly Father!

Brother Zach finished preaching, then prayed in a booming voice that Sadie felt down to her toes.

"That was so good!" whispered Mary. "It makes me want to be a preacher."

"And I could travel around with you and sing," said Sadie.

"Can you sing well?" asked Mary.

"No," said Sadie, giggling. "Can you preach well?"

Mary fell against Sadie and giggled hard.

The campfire burned low, but people sat around talking. Nobody wanted to leave. Sadie knew some of the people went weeks without seeing another person, so when they got together they soaked it all in to remember during the long lonely times.

Just then Kara crept to Sadie's side and sat with her and Mary. "Do you see Sven?" Kara asked in a low voice.

"He left," said Mary.

"But I saw him return," said Kara. "Now I don't see him."

Sadie looked around, but couldn't make out anyone in the dim light from the campfire. "Why won't you talk to him?" asked Sadie.

Kara was quiet so long that Sadie didn't think she was going to answer. "I have some things to work out first," she finally said.

"With Red Colvin?" asked Sadie.

"Yes," said Kara stiffly.

Sadie wanted to ask a dozen questions, but

she bit them all back. It wasn't proper to do. "I'll help you if you want, Kara," Sadie said softly.

"So will I," said Mary.

"Thank you both." Kara cleared her throat and wiped at her eyes. "I'm going to crawl in the tent now before Sven tries to find me again."

"Will you talk to him tomorrow?" asked Sadie.

"Yes . . . And I will marry him if he still wants me." Kara said good night and crept to the tent and crawled inside where Sadie knew Helen was already fast asleep.

"There is a mystery going on," said Mary. "I wonder what it is."

"So do I. Maybe we'll find out tomorrow."

"Tomorrow's the last day of Vida Days." Mary sounded sad.

"I know." Sadie sighed. "It's fun to see everything and everybody, but I will be glad to go home. But I'll miss you, Mary."

"I'll miss you! Sometimes it's hard with just me and Jewel and Malachi. At least you have brothers and sisters."

"And cousins," said Sadie, wrinkling her nose. Just what had made Gerda suddenly turn quiet and not leave the camp? Maybe she'd find that out tomorrow too. Tomorrow was going to be a very full day.

"Good night, Sadie," said Mary, hugging Sadie tightly.

"See you tomorrow, Mary."

Mary ran to Jewel so they could go to their wagon for the night.

Sadie yawned, then yawned again. Suddenly she realized the black cloud she'd been wrapped in was gone. She had been in the presence of her Heavenly Father, and the cloud had vanished!

"Thank You, Father," Sadie whispered. "I love You! I'm glad I belong to You."

12

Important Decisions

Just after breakfast Gerda whispered to Bess—Sadie's Momma, "I have to get away to think by myself. Please don't worry about me. This time I won't do anything foolish."

Bess glanced at Caleb, then back at Gerda. "Be very careful. We don't want Nash Hubert to try anything. Caleb looked for him yesterday, but couldn't find him."

"Maybe he left town," whispered Gerda with a shiver.

"Maybe. But he might be on the lookout for you." Bess brushed Gerda's black hair back and smiled. "I don't want anything to happen to my young Michigan cousin."

Tears stung Gerda's eyes. She couldn't believe Bess could actually love her after the way she'd acted. "Please don't send Sadie after me. I promise to take care of myself."

Bess nodded.

Gerda slipped quietly away from the York family. Sadie had been so deep in thought, she didn't notice.

Gerda walked between tents and around wagons. Last night when she couldn't sleep she'd decided it was time to admit to her age and to act it, no matter what her ma said. Now Gerda was more determined than ever. Yesterday she'd almost ruined her life over a yellow parasol! She groaned as she stopped at the giant cottonwood beside the creek. She honestly hadn't realized the trouble her actions could get her into. If Sadie and Mary hadn't rescued her, she'd be on her way south to Oklahoma with Nash Hubert! Gerda trembled.

She leaned back against the giant cottonwood and watched a green frog slide into the creek and swim across it. Further down the creek three women were filling their pails with water. Several boys were feeding the horses inside the rope corral. This was the last day of Vida Days, and Gerda felt the excitement in the air. Today was the quilt judging contest that both Bess and Opal had entered. Today was the final shoot of the sharpshooter contest. Today she had to give Gabe an answer to his marriage proposal.

Last night she'd watched him perform in front of the entire camp. He'd enjoyed playing his dulcimer and singing the songs. He was never frightened of anything. He was short and wiry, but he seemed like he was as big as Caleb.

Gerda sighed. She was frightened of almost everything. Back in Michigan she'd been all right until Ma had decided she had to say she was thirteen instead of seventeen.

Just then she saw Levi Cass getting his mare from the corral. Gerda eased around the tree until she was out of sight. She couldn't face Levi after what she'd done to him. But she couldn't help it that her love for him had suddenly died. Maybe she wasn't capable of loving anyone. All the Yorks were full of love. Maybe it was because they loved God and put Him first in their lives.

Tears slipped down Gerda's cheek. Could she learn to put God first in her life? Last night she'd listened to the singing and the preaching. She knew if she had to either bow to an idol or be pitched into a fiery furnace, she'd bow.

With an unsteady hand she brushed away her tears. The preacher had said anything she put before God was an idol in her life. She put a lot of things before God. But no longer! "Jesus, I need Your help so I won't bow to any idols. I do want You to be my Savior, and, God, I want You to be my Heavenly Father. Forgive me of all the bad things I've done, and help me to be like You!"

Gerda prayed a while longer. She felt clean and fresh. She smiled. Wouldn't the Yorks be happy about the change in her? Especially Caleb. He'd been losing patience with her, and she didn't blame him a bit.

Just then Gerda saw Caleb walking alone toward town. "I'll talk to Caleb now," she muttered, her heart racing. Sometimes it wasn't easy talking to him. She couldn't wrap him around her little finger like she did other people.

Her gingham skirt flipped around her ankles as Gerda hurried along the path after Caleb. His steps were long. She could tell by the way he walked that he was used to riding horseback. She walked faster in order to catch him before he went inside a store.

She lifted her skirts and ran. Just as she started past the livery Nash Hubert stepped from behind a big haystack and gripped her arm. He clamped a hand over her mouth and dragged her behind the haystack.

"Now I got you!" he hissed. "This time you won't get away!"

Gerda's heart turned over, and her blood ran cold. If only Caleb would come to her rescue! But she knew he wasn't thinking about her. Oh, why couldn't she take care of herself?

She smelled Hubert's sweat and tasted his salty skin as he whispered all the plans he had for her. Silently she prayed for help.

Suddenly a strength she'd never felt before rose up inside her. She did not have to stay Hubert's prisoner! She opened her mouth and sank her teeth deep into the fleshy part of his hand. He cried out and jerked away from her. She spun and rammed him in the stomach with her head, sending him flying back into the hay.

"Don't ever touch me again!" she cried, her cheeks red and her eyes flashing. She spun around and raced back to the path, silently thanking God for His help.

With her head high, Gerda walked down the wooden sidewalk to find Caleb.

Just outside the boardinghouse Kara Lazlow dashed tears from her eyes. She had to talk to Red one more time. Oh, why was he being so stubborn?

Kara slipped inside the boardinghouse and peeked through the door of the dining room. Red wasn't there, but Quint Largo was. She ducked back before he saw her.

No one was at the desk, so Kara slipped upstairs. She'd been to Red's room twice already and knew right where it was. Today was her last chance. After today she'd be married to Sven if he still wanted her and Red would be on his way to another town to repair guns and enter yet another sharpshooter contest.

She tapped on his door and waited, holding her breath. Maybe she should've told little Sadie York her problem. Red took to Sadie like he'd never taken to anyone before. He might listen to her.

Finally Red opened the door. His shirt was half-buttoned, and his wide suspenders hung down the sides of his pant legs. His feet were bare. Impatiently he shook his head, then stepped aside for her to enter. "You might as well not say it," he said as he stabbed his fingers through his red hair, then trailed a finger down the white scar.

Kara sank to the only chair in the room and primly folded her hands in her lap. "Uncle Drew, Grandpa is sorry!"

Red frowned. "I told you not to call me that!"

"You're my uncle! A very stubborn one, I might add." Kara sighed heavily. "Grandpa is old, and he wants to see you."

"He should've known better than to send you." Red buttoned his shirt, pulled his suspenders up in place, and slipped on his socks.

"I told you he didn't send me. He doesn't know where you are. I found out accidentally." Kara brushed a strand of light brown hair off her flushed cheek.

"I heard talk that you came as a mail-order bride."

Kara lifted her chin. "What if I did?"

Red wagged his finger at her. "You could've had anybody you wanted in Chicago. I say you came here to get away from the family."

"What if I did?"

He leaned down to her. "So don't try sendin' me back where I don't want to go!"

"Uncle Drew . . ." Kara stopped. ". . . Red, the family does try to run our lives. I know that. But Grandpa is old. He's your father! You could at least make peace with him before he dies."

"He don't want to make peace," said Red as he sank to the edge of the unmade bed. The warm wind blew the curtain at the open window. "I didn't want to tell you, but I will."

Kara's stomach tightened. "What?"

"Papa sent Largo after me." Red rubbed the scar. "He found me six years ago and did this to me. And now he came after me again. Papa doesn't want to make peace with me. He wants me dead."

Kara gasped and shook her head. "I can't believe that!"

"Ask Quint Largo."

"Maybe he's lying, Uncle Drew. Did you ever think of that?"

Red sprang up and paced the small room. "Why would he lie? What's in it for him?"

"He could be on Granger's payroll instead of Grandpa's. Cousin Granger doesn't want you back in Chicago because he's afraid you'd take over the business."

Red stopped short. "You could be right, little niece." Red slipped on his leather vest and hooked his gunbelt around his hips, then pulled on his boots. "Granger always did want to run the business. He does have a good business head, even if he don't know about turning out a decent gun. He's got others that know how. I'm happy as a gunsmith out here in the wide-open prairie."

Kara walked to Red and put her hand on his arm. "Uncle Drew, please go see Grandpa. You don't have to set foot in the business or see Granger. But see Grandpa. Set it straight with him. He cares about you."

A muscle jumped in Red's jaw. "I just might do that before the snow flies. Now, how about this mail-order bride thing I heard about?"

Kara flushed. She told him about corresponding with Sven Johnson for several months, then agreeing to marry him. "When I learned about you being here, I said I'd come if we could marry during Vida Days. I wanted you to be with me at the wedding."

Red wrapped his arms around Kara and held her tight. "I don't know what made me change my mind, but I have."

"Sadie York said she was praying for us," said Kara.

Red grinned. "I'll be switched!"

"I must find Sven now and see if the wedding is on for tonight after the shooting contest."

Red tapped the tip of Kara's nose with his finger. "You have a right good chance to win that contest."

Kara grinned. "I know. You're the one who taught me to shoot."

"Little Sadie York is mighty good too."

"She sure is." Kara laughed up at Red. "Maybe she'll beat us both."

13
Revenge

Laughing, Sadie dodged away before Web could tag her and make her It. Town kids and country kids were playing together for the first time since Vida Days had started. Shouts and laughter rang across the endless prairie. Sadie was glad Momma had said she didn't have to be concerned about Gerda. It felt good not to hunt down Gerda and save her from whatever trouble she got herself into.

Web shouted and ran after Sadie even though he knew he'd never catch her. She could run faster than anyone except Good One. Web longed to be able to run faster or shoot straighter than Sadie, but he knew he probably never would.

Finally Web turned away from Sadie and ran after one of the town kids.

Sadie stopped and let the wind dry her sweat. She retied her bonnet, blocking out the sun.

"Pssst . . . Sadie York!"

Sadie spun around with a frown. Finally she spotted someone hiding in the tall grass. It was Melinda, one of the town girls. Sadie tensed. "What do you want?"

"Come here."

Sadie hesitated, then walked toward Melinda. She looked as if she'd been crying. Dirt streaked her muslin dress. One hair bow was missing, and the other one hung down her thin shoulder.

Melinda led Sadie around a knoll, out of sight of the others. "I hate to ask you to help me, but I knew you'd be the only one that would."

"Help you what?" asked Sadie suspiciously.

Melinda patted her flushed cheeks and looked worried. "Jake and Harvey took Amy out on the prairie and just left her because they were mad at her. I tried to go after her, but they chased me back."

"Get Amy's pa to help."

"She'd be in big trouble if he knew what happened. He told her to stay home and go out only with her mother." Melinda blinked tears away. "Nobody else will help me. But you're a good Christian girl, and I know you'll help."

Sadie sighed heavily. "What do you want me to do?"

"Ride with me after Amy. I have the buggy. I'm scared to go by myself in case the boys try to stop me again."

Sadie's head spun. Should she go or shouldn't she? What if it was a trick? But what if it wasn't? Melinda did look frightened and in need of help. Finally Sadie decided it was only right to help. She didn't want the town kids to think she'd hold a grudge. "I'll go. But you know I have to be right back because of the sharpshooter contest."

Melinda waved her hand as if to dismiss the whole thing. "We got lots of time."

A few minutes later Sadie sat in the single seat buggy pulled by one horse while Melinda drove. Sadie wondered where Amy would sit, but shrugged off the thought. Several times Sadie glanced back the way they'd come. Caleb had taught her to always look back and read the hills so she could always find her way back. Melinda probably knew the way, but Sadie didn't want to take a chance.

The hot sun burned down on Sadie, and the hot wind seemed to scorch right through her dress and bonnet. Her mouth was dry, and she longed for a long, cold drink straight from the well.

"It's not much further," said Melinda.

"Maybe she started walking back and got lost," said Sadie.

Melinda shook her head. "She'd never do that! I hope she didn't. It would be awful to get lost in the prairie. Wolves . . . Coyotes . . . Rattlesnakes . . . No water . . . No shelter from the sun."

"Amy must really be scared!"

"I bet so too." Melinda looked at Sadie. "Would you be scared?"

"Yes."

Finally Melinda pulled up. She looked around with a frown. "I thought she'd be right here. Jake said it was where the two big blowouts were. See?" She pointed to the sides of the hills that the wind had completely blown away. "I'll go look around the other side." Melinda jumped to the ground. "Coming?"

115

Sadie nodded and followed Melinda. A hawk soared in the endless blue sky. Bees buzzed around yellow flowers. But there was no sign of Amy. "Maybe she went that way," said Sadie, pointing east. "I see two blowouts over there."

"We'll go see," said Melinda. "Wait! I'll drive over there, and you check around that hill."

Sadie looked to where Melinda pointed, then nodded. Sadie walked around the hill while Melinda ran back to the buggy.

Sadie found a badger's hole and a carcass of a calf, but she didn't find Amy.

Just then Melinda shouted from the buggy, "I hope you never find your way back, Sadie York! I'm leaving you all alone! Amy's at home right where she belongs!"

Sadie's heart sank as Melinda laughed loud and long. "Don't leave me!" cried Sadie as she raced toward the buggy, but Melinda whipped the horse into a mad run. The buggy swayed dangerously and was soon out of sight around a low hill.

Sadie stopped dead in her tracks. Blood roared in her ears, and she clenched and unclenched her fists. "How could I be so dumb?" Frowning, she looked off in the direction Melinda had driven. Was Melinda deliberately going in the wrong direction to fool her into walking that way? Or was Melinda going to get herself lost out on the prairie?

Shielding her eyes against the glare of the sun, Sadie looked up at the sun to see the time. It was already late in the afternoon. Just how long would it take her to get back to town? Would she get there before the sharpshooter contest?

Anger raged inside her. How she wanted to find the town kids and beat them all up. "No. I can't do that," she said with a firm shake of her head. Oh, but she wanted to! Right now it was very hard to do what Jesus wanted her to do! "Jesus, I know You don't want me to get angry or take revenge on the town kids, so I won't. Help me get back to town safely and on time." Sadie bit her lower lip. She sighed heavily. "And, Jesus, help Melinda get back to town safely too."

Sadie ran in the direction they'd come. Suddenly she stopped. Maybe Melinda had circled around when they'd driven out and now was heading straight back toward town.

Just then the grass at Sadie's feet parted, and a blue racer as big around as her wrist tasted the air with its needle-thin tongue. Her heart in her mouth, Sadie jumped back, then stood still to let the snake slither past.

Sadie took a deep, steadying breath, then ran up a hill, careful of each step she took in case the entire top of the hill was blown away. When they'd first moved to the edge of the sandhills, Helen had fallen into a blowout and couldn't get out by herself. Sadie had tied her bonnet string to her apron string and dropped it down for Helen. Helen had grabbed the makeshift rope and climbed up out of the blowout, leaving behind a small landslide of sand. Sadie knew if she fell in a deep blowout now, no one would know where to look for her to pull her out.

The top of the hill was solid, and Sadie stood there and looked all around. She couldn't see even a dot on the prairie that could be Melinda in the buggy. Sadie spotted the hills she'd marked with her eye on the way, and she ran down the hill and toward those hills. Her lips felt cracked and dry. Her throat ached for a drink of cold water.

Finally she slowed to a walk. She lifted her

head and shouted, "You town kids can't beat me! I will find my way back to Vida, and I will shoot the best I can in the contest!"

The words seemed to hang in the air, then were blown away by the hot wind.

14

The Champion Sharpshooter

Sadie watched the sun sink even lower as she ran toward Vida. She refused to let herself think about being too late or too tired for the shoot. She would make it! She would shoot her very best!

Suddenly she heard voices up ahead around a hill. She stopped, her chest heaving. Jake's deep voice and Melinda's shrill laugh drifted to her. The town kids were just on the other side of the hill! They were probably waiting to waylay her just in case she made it this far. She'd fool them! She inched around the hill, then sank down into the tall grass. Once before she'd crawled on her stomach across the Hepfords' yard to stop two Indians from shooting that family. Once again she'd crawl on her stomach until she was past the town kids. They'd never expect that of her. She thought of the snakes and ants and other creeping things deep in the grass. A chill ran down her spine, and she hesitated.

Sadie sank down flat on her stomach. The grass scratched her face and tickled her nose. A grasshopper landed on her hand, spit its tobacco on her, then hopped off. Her stomach turned. She rubbed the dark juice off her hand and inched forward. Just how much time would it take to get past the town kids? She dare not think of that now.

She heard the town kids talking about the fun they'd have the last night of Vida Days. Sadie turned her head slightly. She saw the town kids, but there wasn't a horse or buggy in sight. Were the kids on foot?

Sadie smiled. Now she'd change her plans. She'd outrun the kids! Back in Douglas County she'd outrun even the big eighth-grade boys. She would've outrun everyone the day of the race two days ago if she hadn't stopped to help Good One. She knew she could outrun these kids.

Suddenly she leaped to her feet and let out a wild cowboy yell. She saw the fear on all the kids' faces before she sprang forward and sped toward town, her feet barely touching the ground.

"Get her, Jake!" Amy yelled. "You can do it!"

Sadie didn't dare look back or she'd lose stride. She ran like she'd never run before. She ran faster than the day she'd run from Mitch to keep from kissing him for the box of paper she'd desperately wanted.

Up ahead she spotted the tents and the wagons, the tall cottonwoods and the corral. She ran further and saw the crowd gathered for the shooting match. Her lungs burned, but she kept running. A pain stabbed her side, but she ignored it.

She thought about her rifle in the back of the wagon, but hoped Kara would've gotten it already.

Just then the crowd at the shooting range turned to watch her run. A tingle went down her spine and she almost lost stride, but she kept running while the crowd cheered her on.

Caleb broke away from the others and ran to meet her. Her legs suddenly gave way and she started to fall, but he caught her and lowered her to the ground.

"Somebody get water for her!" shouted Red Colvin, running to her side.

Sadie gasped for air, struggling to pull enough into her lungs to breathe again.

Red kept the others from crowding in on her.

"It's time for the shoot," said Taylor Jennings.

Red looked up at him from Sadie's side. "If you want to start it now, you'll have to count me out."

"Me too," said El and Kara.

Quint Largo only grunted.

"We can't wait too long or the light will be bad," said Jennings.

"She'll be fine soon," said Caleb, wiping Sadie's face off with his handkerchief. He helped her drink a sip of water, then waited until she could drink more. "Later you can tell me what happened out there," he said for her ears alone.

She nodded. Finally she sat up. "I'm all right now," she said hoarsely. She glanced around the crowd, and her eyes fell on the town kids. She saw the fear on their faces. She turned away from them without telling on them.

"Kara has your rifle," said Caleb.

Sadie smiled at Kara.

"Maybe we can get this contest under way now," said Taylor Jennings impatiently.

The crowd walked back to the range as Sadie stood up. Her legs felt like water, and she almost dropped to the ground again.

Caleb picked her up like she was Baby Joey and carried her high in his arms.

"We'll tell the mayor to have you shoot last," said Red.

Sadie smiled at him, and he winked at her.

A minute later Taylor Jennings stood before the crowd and told the rules of the sharpshooter contest. This time the shooters would shoot one at a time at three targets that were even further away. The bull's-eye blurred before Sadie's eyes, and she blinked until it was in focus.

"The winner is the one who gets their shots the closest to the center of each bull's-eye," said Jennings. "If there's a tie, the shooter moves further away from the target. May the best man . . . or the best Annie Oakley . . . win."

The crowd clapped and cheered.

Just then Sadie saw Largo pull out a knife and start to stab Red Colvin. "Red!" cried Sadie as she lunged forward and bumped Largo off balance.

Red spun around as Largo leaped up, his knife poised and his knees bent.

"Drop the knife or I'll shoot," barked Caleb, his Colt .45 in his hand, aimed right at Largo's heart.

Largo glanced at Caleb, hesitated, and finally dropped the knife. "I'll get you next time, Colvin!" snarled Largo.

"No, you won't," said Joshua Cass as he caught Largo's hands and tied them securely. "I'm going to lock you up right now, and tomorrow you'll be on your way down to jail in Grand Island."

"I mean to have a long talk with him before he leaves," said Red, his eyes narrowed.

"What's gonna happen next?" asked Taylor Jennings, scratching his head. "That leaves us with only four shooters. Let's get on with it. I call Kara Lazlow up first."

Kara smiled at Sadie, then up at Red. With Sadie's rifle in her hands, Kara stepped to the mark.

"Fire when ready," said Jennings.

Kara snapped the rifle to her shoulder, aimed, and fired. She levered in a new shell, aimed at the next target, and fired. She took a deep breath, levered in another shell, aimed at the third target, and fired. She stepped back and handed the rifle to Sadie. "Good luck," Kara said.

Davis Greavy took Kara's targets down and put new ones up as Jennings called for El Hepford.

His face red, El stepped to the line. The crowd grew silent, and El's shots rang out.

Red was next. He smiled down at Sadie. "I'd like to see you win, little mite, but I aim to shoot my best anyhow."

"I'm glad," said Sadie with a wide smile.

The crowd hushed as Red stepped to the line. He stood tall and straight, the full sleeves of his plaid shirt blowing in the wind.

"Fire when ready," said Jennings softly.

Red shot fast and straight, then stepped back with a loud war whoop that made Sadie laugh.

Caleb squeezed Sadie's arm. "God is with you," he whispered.

Sadie smiled.

"Sadie York!" called Jennings.

The crowd cheered and whistled.

Sadie stepped to the line. Her legs felt strong,

and she felt ready. Once again she was going to shoot her very best.

"Fire when ready," said Jennings.

Sweat stung Sadie's eye, and she wiped it away with the sleeve of her dress.

"Little Annie Oakley!" yelled someone from the crowd.

This time it didn't bother Sadie. If she could shoot as well as Annie Oakley, she'd win the contest.

Sadie lifted her rifle to her shoulder, aimed, and fired. She levered the next shell in, aimed, and fired. Her hand trembled slightly as she levered in the last shell. Silently she prayed for a steady hand and a sure eye. She took a deep breath, snapped the rifle to her shoulder, aimed, and fired.

The crowd roared. Red tugged Sadie's braid and said, "You done real good, little mite."

"I'm proud of you, Sadie Rose," said Caleb softly.

Sadie smiled at him, her heart bursting with love for him. Soon she'd know if she had won the Winchester '76 for him.

While they waited for the judges to check the targets Sadie saw Kara walk up to Sven. Sven blushed to the roots of his blond hair.

"Hello, Sven," said Kara very properly. "I am sorry I couldn't speak to you sooner, but I had to deal with a family problem." She motioned to Red Colvin. "This is my uncle, and he needed my help."

Sadie blinked in surprise. So that was the secret between Kara and Red!

Sven shook hands with Red. "I was afraid you were my competition," said Sven, grinning.

"Not me," said Red, chuckling. "You're gettin' a

mighty headstrong lady. I hope you know how to handle her better than I do."

Kara blushed. "We can talk after a while about our plans, Sven."

"I asked the preacher to stay until noon tomorrow," said Sven. "If you want to wait longer, he'll be in Jake's Crossing in two weeks. Bess York offered to let you bed down with them if you choose to do that."

Kara laughed. "You have it all taken care of, don't you?"

Sven flushed again. "Not a house yet. I thought you might not come."

"I came. But I can't live without a house," said Kara.

Sadie smiled. She knew everyone would work hard and fast to build a sod house for Kara and Sven. That meant one less fine young man for Opal to consider marrying.

Just then Taylor Jennings called them all to order. "We have a winner!" he shouted.

Sadie's mouth turned bone-dry, and butterflies fluttered wildly in her stomach. She reached for Caleb's big hand and held on tight.

"We know all four of these folks are real sharpshooters," said Jennings. "But the champion sharpshooter this year is . . . Sadie York!"

Sadie sagged against Caleb while the crowd cheered.

"She's as good as Little Sure Shot herself," said Jennings proudly.

Red Colvin lifted Sadie high in a bear hug, Kara kissed her cheek, and El shook her hand. Momma and the family crowded close and congratulated Sadie. Taylor Jennings presented her with the Winchester '76, and she held it proudly.

She almost pinched herself to see if she had fallen asleep out on the prairie and was dreaming it all.

Much later Sadie found Caleb alone, and she carried the Winchester to him. "Daddy, I won this for you," she said softly.

"Sadie Rose," he said in surprise, "that rifle is yours fair and square."

"I know. But I want you to have it because you're the best daddy in the world and I don't want you to ever feel stuck with us."

Caleb rested the rifle against the wagon and took both of Sadie's hands in his. "Sadie Rose York, I love you. I love all of you. And I'd never feel stuck with you. What ever gave you such an idea?"

Sadie bit her lip, then told him what she'd overheard.

Caleb grinned and glanced around to make sure no one could hear him. "Sadie Rose, I sure wasn't speakin' of you young 'uns. It was the Taskers, especially Gerda, I had in mind. They try my patience."

Sadie's heart leaped with joy. She pulled her hands free and hugged Caleb so tight she hurt her arms on his gun belt. "I love you, Daddy!" She let him go and whispered, "I get mighty tired of the Taskers too."

"Gerda hasn't had a chance to tell you, Sadie Rose, but she's a different young lady now. She asked Jesus to be her Savior. And she even told me the truth about her age. She and Gabe are gonna talk to her ma and pa about them gettin' married in the fall."

Sadie gasped in surprise. God had worked a lot of miracles during Vida Days, and she knew He wasn't finished yet.

"Come on, my little champion sharpshooter,"

said Caleb. "I'll put our rifle away for now. Let's go listen to the singin' and playin' at the Hepford wagon."

Sadie watched Caleb put their Winchester in the back of the wagon. Then she put her hand in his and walked across the camp to the Hepfords', singing in her heart the whole way.